CAT O' NINE TALES

BY

KRYSTAL LAWRENCE

For Cassidy —
Best wishes —
Krystal Lawrence

TELEMACHUS PRESS

Cover designed by Telemachus Press, LLC

Cover art:
Copyright © iStock/50088806/powerofforever
Copyright © iStock/23016283/mark wragg
Copyright © iStock/20274022/glenkar
Copyright © istockphoto.com/eszawa

Interior art by Kira Sokolovskaia

Scene changes:
    Cabin: Copyright © iStock/13147998/ZargonDesign
    Gun: Copyright © iStock/5166677/browndogstudios
    Crow: Copyright © OpenClipArt/drunken_duck
    Cowboy Boot: Copyright © OpenClipArt/bnsonger47
    Cat: Copyright © OpenClipArt/molumen
    Flying Saucer: Copyright © iStock/75923779/koya79
    Man and Woman: Copyright © Shutterstock_93860536
    Dog: Copyright © ClipArtQueen.com/Jumping Wolf
    Politician: Copyright © OpenClipArt/j4p4n
    Potient Bottle: Copyright © iStock/9193473; iStock/5414434/old-photographic-chemical-bottle
    Interlocked Rings: Copyright © iStock/26197535/Mathier
    Statue: Copyright © iStock/12393212/Jitalia17
    Gavel: Copyright © iStock/60433788/thumbnail/Katsapura

Published by Telemachus Press, LLC
http://www.telemachuspress.com

As the Crow Flies was first published, September, 2016 by Sanitarium Magazine, Burgess Hill, UK

Visit the author website:
http://www.darksidestories.com

ISBN: 978-1-942899-98-3 (eBook)
ISBN: 978-1-942899-99-0 (Hardcover)

Version 2016.08.21

10 9 8 7 6 5 4 3 2 1

For Mom, Jan & Anya....
You color my world beautiful

TABLE OF CONTENTS

THE PERFECT CRIME

CLAUDE WINSTON WAS a man with few redeeming qualities. He was possessed of superior intelligence and was a sharp dresser. Apart from those two attributes, there was absolutely nothing praiseworthy to be said of the man.

Few people knew this however, because Claude always put on a very socially acceptable demeanor, and could charm both men and women alike. In short, he had everyone snowed, including his wife.

Julia Winston was the polar opposite of the man she married. Though she was born into great wealth, Julia was kind-hearted, well-mannered, and always willing to help those less fortunate. She was generous, soft-spoken and exceptionally pretty.

Claude had, of course, married Julia for her money. For the first year he found living with her tolerable. However, the honeymoon ended quickly and within a few short months of the nuptials Julia began to get on his nerves. Eventually, every last detail about his wife drove Claude crazy.

He hated the smell of her perfume, how she chewed her food, the sound her heels made clicking across the polished marble floors in the house, her laugh, and especially the sight of her naked body. She revolted him.

Since Julia's father controlled the money, Claude had to become quite creative when it came to feathering his own nest. He took a job the old man generously offered in the accounting division of his firm, and slowly began embezzling funds into an off-shore account he set up in the Cayman Islands. Never enough money at any one time to raise suspicion was moved, and nothing that could ever be traced back to his desk in the unlikely event someone should become wise to his activity. He had stolen the passwords of three other employees, and all illegal transactions were performed from their computers after hours.

Julia had a terrible phobia of flying and did not like to travel. Claude, on the other hand, enjoyed taking frequent trips. Julia never stood in his way or complained about these sojourns. She trusted Claude, and never imagined him to be the cheating kind, so was unworried when he jetted off to some distant port without her for a little R&R.

Julia was correct in assuming that her husband was not unfaithful. He was smart enough to know that should he ever get caught with his hand up another woman's skirt, Julia's father would put an end to the marriage, the Mercedes, the mansion, and most of all, the money.

He would lose his reputation as a stellar gentleman among the town's elite, and ruin everything he had been working toward so carefully.

Claude knew almost from the day he married Julia that he was going to kill her. He could not divorce her because of the concrete and brick pre-nup agreement her father insisted he sign before he would allow the nuptials to take place. If Claude ever left Julia, he would leave penniless.

Four years into the marriage a daughter was born. Two years later, a son. Claude felt little affection for his children, but performed the expected tasks of a dedicated father, as an actor would perform a high-paying role in a film. He took great pains to make sure that his wife, his children, and especially his father-in-law were always convinced of his devotion. Claude spent thirteen long years playing the part flawlessly and planning the perfect crime.

It took that long for him to make sure there was enough money in the offshore account to safely disappear with. Once comfortable with the nest egg, he saw to the few other details he needed to implement in order to safely carry out his plan. A new identification, complete with passport and credit cards was obtained. A non-descript, five-year old white Prius was purchased from a Craig's List ad with cash and street-parked a mile from his home. He moved it to a different location every day.

Lastly, a small cabin in the woods he would escape to, nestled so deep into the tangled forest it was not on any map, was purchased discreetly from the surviving relative of a recluse who lived there for the last thirty years of his life. There was no real estate agent involved, and the relative lived in Montana. It was a cash deal and he never met the seller face to face. The key was left under a rock on the porch for prospective buyers to view the property. Claude found the ad in a distant town's local newspaper. He waited for six months after it stopped running to respond, keeping the small ad tucked into his wallet all that time. Claude was the only person who ever responded. The seller asked few questions, so happy was he to finally unload the unwanted bit of rundown real estate.

The murder of Julia Winston would be the perfect crime. The key element to his successful escape was the getaway.

Once the plan was in place Claude practiced driving to the secluded cabin he had purchased deep in the woods. The problem was he kept getting lost trying to find it after dark. Once, he spent an alarming forty-five minutes babying the Prius out of a muddy trench it was trapped in after one wrong, and nearly lethal turn.

He had no intention of killing his wife in broad daylight and then casually pulling out of the driveway and cruising through town and onto the highway. The murder had to take place at night and very shortly after they retired for the evening, insuring Julia would not be found until morning, and giving Claude at least six hours to attend to every last detail of covering his tracks and disappearing to the cloistered cabin in the woods.

At this point, after numerous failed attempts to find the cabin after nightfall, Claude enlisted the help of an accomplice. Her name was Greta.

Greta stood for Global Repositioning Enhanced Tracking Apparatus; a state of the art GPS system Claude purchased from a mail order military supply company. It had far advanced technology than anything available to civilians. Claude programmed Greta, turn by turn, to his hideaway in the woodlands one rainy afternoon.

It would be Greta's job to see he made a clean getaway and reached the pre-arranged destination of his escape quickly and cleanly, with no wrong turns.

Claude and Greta performed several late-night practice drills before he carried out his plan. There could be no room for error.

Claude knew that as the spouse he would immediately fall under suspicion when his wife was found dead. He was smart enough to know that he would not be able to convince a savvy detective of his innocence. The prisons were full of people who thought they could outwit the police. Claude was too smart for that. He planned to never sit in an interrogation room and attempt such foolishness. He would be long gone by then.

Perhaps everyone would know "whodunit," they would just never be able to find him. Greta would see to it he reached the cabin, where he had stocked enough provisions to survive for nine months.

After the authorities stopped feverishly searching for him is when he would board a plane to his new life abroad. He was thinking Tuscany. Claude fancied himself quite the wine connoisseur. There was time to decide what exotic port he would next call home. He would have nine months to figure it out.

Why so long? Because Claude knew the world had become over-run with surveillance cameras. They were everywhere. He would be seen and arrested at the airport if he attempted to board a plane right away. He estimated nine months to be enough time for law enforcement to stop scanning the airports, bus terminals and train stations for him with such a keen eye.

The only place local law enforcement would ever see his face after Julia was dead would be on the evening news for a brief time while the story was still alive in the media. Before long, Claude knew, the next heinous crime would steal the attention away from Julia's murder.

After Julia was dead, Claude Winston would be dead, too. It was Emille Veragasi, complete with all the correct papers, who would emerge from the cabin nine months later. There was enough black hair dye to last for a year in the cabinet under the bathroom sink to cover his sandy blond hair, and at least one hundred pair of brown contact lenses to cover his blue eyes. There were also four complete sets of Rosetta Stone learning CDs. Emille would use the time wisely to become proficient in Italian, Spanish, French and German before leaving the cabin behind. After thirteen years of planning, nothing could possibly go wrong.

Without hesitation on the night Claude planned to carry out his crime, he offered to bring Julia a nightcap. She favored a warmed snifter of Remy Martin before bedtime.

He heated the libation to the temperature of her liking and then crushed six prescription sleeping tablets into the brandy. It tasted only slightly bitter when he placed a brandy-dipped finger against his tongue. Adding another two ounces of Remy solved the problem. He wasn't worried about what the toxicology report would reveal after her autopsy. Everyone would know he'd done it. That was of no concern to him.

"Thank you, darling," his wife said taking the warm glass from her husband's hand.

Claude kissed her goodnight and lay down beside her in the bed. He waited until she was snoring softly an hour later before rising and placing a pillow over Julia's face.

She awoke only briefly, struggling weakly for less than a minute before it was over and she lay still. Claude kept the pillow in place for ten minutes after Julia stopped moving. Once he removed it, he checked her carefully for a pulse. Satisfied, he dressed quickly, and five minutes later was jogging from the house in the direction where he had parked the Prius.

Two hours later, when he was deep into the forest, and by his calculations less than an hour from the cabin, the left front headlight winked out on the Prius. Enveloped by the overgrown trees, Claude noticed the darkened headlight immediately. He was comforted to hear Greta's soothing voice instruct him to turn left in four hundred feet. She did not need the headlights to see where she was going.

Claude didn't know why, but suddenly after the Prius's headlight died the forest began to feel strange. The trees seemed closer to the narrow path he was driving on. He heard the ominous scrape of branches against the right side of the car. He wasn't frightened.

Shortly after hearing the branches scrape that first time, they became a constant rasping against the car, as though they were trying to scratch some chronic itch, or maybe claw their way inside.

Claude was reminded of a book his children enjoyed where the trees came to life and grabbed people. He thought it might have been one of the Harry Potter stories, but couldn't be sure. He never paid very close attention to anything he read to the kids while playing the dutiful dad.

The terrain grew steeper and Claude was forced to accelerate harder to negotiate the incline. Soon his ears were popping as though the altitude had changed. He could not recall ever having that happen on any of the practice trips.

Shortly after that, the radio reception departed and he was left with only static all the way across the dial. Now all he had to keep him company was the sound of the wind sighing through the claustrophobic trees, and the reassuring voice of Greta advising him every so often to turn right or left.

Thank God for Greta, Claude thought. While they had made this same journey a dozen times in anticipation of this very evening, Claude reasoned that it had all been a rehearsal. He believed the trees probably scraped the car on the previous trips as well, and he must not have heard them. The incline must have altered, but perhaps he was more aware of it tonight because the car had become half blind.

Tonight his nerves were heightened due to the fact that he had finally carried out the plan to murder Julia after over a decade of planning. That's why he was suddenly so painfully aware of the nearness of the trees and every previously unnoticed bump in the rough terrain. Even the moon seemed eerily bright.

As for the radio, he couldn't recall if he had been listening to it or not when they did the practice runs to the cabin. It was possible that he just didn't have it on during those previous excursions, so was unaware of it when the reception was lost.

Claude was not a man given easily to fright. He only began to feel something close to dismay when he glanced at his watch and realized that he had been driving at least twenty minutes longer than he should have been. It had never taken Greta this long to get him to the cabin before.

"Come on, baby, don't fail me now. Not tonight," he pleaded lovingly to the GPS.

Greta responded at once. "Turn left in four hundred feet."

Claude breathed a sigh of relief and made the turn. Her soothing voice advised him, "Your destination is ahead two hundred feet."

"That's my girl," Claude said, when to his horror, he suddenly plummeted over a jagged cliff and down a steep saw-toothed mountainside into the ravine fifty feet below.

As Claude screamed, the car tumbled end over end, mercilessly crashing against the barbed rocks.

The last words he heard were, "You have reached your destination, you bastard."

GOLDSTEIN'S LAST PATIENT

THE WAITING ROOM was done in muted, soothing earth tones. While the carpet wasn't of quality grade, the furnishings were tasteful and the magazines all current issues. Doris listened to the calming piped in Muzak and thought, *God help me. What am I doing here?* The place screamed psychiatrist's office, or should she say, it whispered it, in a pacifying voice reserved exclusively for those presumed unstable.

At precisely 5:00 PM the office door opened and Dr. Goldstein ushered the well-dressed woman inside. He assessed his new patient. She appeared to be in her early to mid-forties and obviously took great care with her appearance. Her hair was expensively cut into a chin-length bob, her makeup carefully applied. The silk blouse and slacks complimented a pleasing figure, and both her purse and scarf touted the logo of famous designers.

There were no surprises when Doris entered the inner sanctum from the waiting room. Same drab colors, same attractive furniture. She was sure there must be a Mrs. Goldstein somewhere. For some reason the doctor didn't strike her as the kind of man with an eye for style.

"Good afternoon, Mrs. Hughes." Goldstein smiled politely. "Please have a seat, or you may lie on the couch if you would be more comfortable."

His handshake was firm and dry. "Nice to meet you. Thank you for fitting me in on such short notice, Doctor." Doris chose the over-stuffed armchair. The couch was just too cliché.

"So," Goldstein began, sitting down across from her in a matching chair. "What brings you here today? You mentioned something about nightmares on the phone. Is that correct?"

Doris looked thoughtfully at the doctor. The couch wasn't the only thing cliché in this office. Goldstein was stroking his neatly trimmed, ginger colored beard thoughtfully, ala Freud. His face was arranged in the perfect expression of polite interest, mild curiosity and great empathy. She wondered how long he had practiced that look before it became second nature to him. It was all she could do not to giggle.

"Before we get into that, I need to know if everything I tell you is completely confidential. Are you like a lawyer? You can't tell anyone anything we talk about?"

Goldstein replied, "Of course. The only exception would be if you are a danger to yourself or others. Then I would be obligated to alert the authorities, or medical personnel."

"Obligated? Is that a legal obligation or a moral one?" she wondered.

The doctor considered her question. "It would be both, don't you think?"

"If I'm a danger, you say? Well, what if the danger has passed? Would you still tell?"

The doctor smiled reassuringly. "For what it's worth, Mrs. Hughes, in all the years I have been practicing, I have never had reason to disclose anything a patient has told me. I take confidentiality very seriously."

This was reassuring. Doris was here because she needed to make a confession. It was the only way she would be able to stop Hank from following her down into sleep every night and haunting her dreams. He refused to stay dead.

While, with the steep price tag on an hour of his time, and a name like Goldstein, this man clearly was not a priest, she thought a shrink would be the next best thing. And maybe he could offer some guidance on how to make Hank slither back down into the stoking fires of Hell where he belonged.

Dr. Goldstein said, "Why don't we start with the basics. Are you married?"

"Yes—to my second husband. But I am not here to talk about Martin."

"Alright, then what would you like to talk about, Mrs. Hughes?"

"It's my first husband. He's haunting me. And now he isn't alone. He's bringing that bitch Charmaine with him."

Goldstein's expression never changed. "Who is Charmaine?"

"She is—I mean she was, my cousin. She's dead. So is Hank for that matter."

"Hank was husband number one, I take it?"

Doris nodded.

"And why is it you think they are haunting you? Maybe you should start at the beginning. With their deaths, perhaps."

"Their deaths aren't the beginning. The beginning was when I married Hank in the first place. He was a terrible husband."

Goldstein smiled encouragingly. Now they were getting somewhere. "What made him terrible?"

Doris launched into the story of her first marriage to Henry Sweeny; a bear of a man with a hair-trigger temper and all sorts of voracious appetites. She described him as a wicked drunk and shameless womanizer. She filled the psychiatrist in on all the ugly particulars of this union. Her details were so vivid Goldstein felt as though he could see the man standing right in front of him. Hank

Sweeney's sinister smile, issuing from a deeply lined ancient mariner face, his unruly hair that never obeyed a comb, his lumbering swagger, his booming voice and ruddy complexion—always red from too much whiskey, and his numerous affairs.

Doris said he treated life like it was one big party, and his wife as if she were there solely for his enjoyment. Then she corrected herself. "Actually," she amended, "he treated everyone like they were only on this earth for his entertainment. It wasn't just me. It was society at large."

Goldstein asked, "You are saying he was immature?"

"No. I'm saying he was an asshole." Her face flushed and she threw her hands up to cover her mouth. "I'm sorry! That just flew out."

Goldstein waved away the apology. "No need to be. Please go on. You can say whatever you want to in here."

Doris laughed shrilly. "Well, he was one. He still is, in fact. What other name is there for a man who couldn't care less if you forgot to buy toilet paper, but would beat the crap out of you with a belt if you came home without his whiskey?"

"May I ask how he died?" Goldstein inquired in a gentle voice.

Doris grimaced. "I'm getting to that. That's why I made this appointment in the first place. You see, I am hoping if I ummm…unburden myself, then maybe he will leave me alone and let me sleep. He stayed away for ten years. Now he's back, and the son of a bitch is bringing Charmaine with him."

"So, this is not the first time you have experienced bad dreams involving Hank?"

"No. He haunted me on and off for the first six years after his death."

"It's not uncommon to have nightmares about people we have lost. Sometimes there is a sense of guilt for surviving relatives, even when they had nothing to do with, or could not change what happened. The passing of a loved one, even a difficult spouse, is never easy. But you must know it's not your fault, Doris. You shouldn't blame yourself."

At this Doris dissolved into hysterical laughter. It was several minutes before she could get herself under control.

Goldstein waited patiently for her to compose herself and go on.

When the last of the giggles trailed off, Doris said, "At first, I told everyone Hank left me for another woman. Given his reputation, no one doubted that story."

"Why didn't you just tell them he had passed?"

A queer light filled her eyes, and the look she gave the doctor was both cunning and deranged. Her voice lowered almost to a whisper. "Because I couldn't. I didn't want anyone to know he was dead."

Goldstein stopped asking questions. He realized he was not going to be able to lead Doris into revealing details. He would have to wait and let her tell her story in her own way and in her own time. She was his last appointment of the day, and he was content to let her talk as long as she needed to, even if they went over the hour she had paid for in cash. Besides, this was getting interesting. He was starting to wonder if this demure, feminine lady might be suffering from some rather serious mental issues. Schizophrenia maybe.

Doris abruptly stopped talking. She pointed to a photo on the wall behind Goldstein's desk. Smiling from the frame was a plain looking woman, two plain looking children, and one really cute dog. Doris asked, "Is that your family?"

He smiled. "Yes."

"They look nice."

Goldstein smiled again but said nothing.

Doris sighed. "So where was I?"

"You were telling me that when Hank died you told everyone he had left you for another woman."

"Oh, right. But later, after about six months, I started thinking about the life insurance. That was money I was entitled to. Money I earned. I spent five long years in Hell being Mrs. Henry Sweeney, and I should be compensated for them. Even though…" she trailed off and would not finish the sentence.

Goldstein waited. He wasn't going to ask her to complete the thought. He knew she wouldn't. She had caught herself saying something she hadn't intended to disclose. Pushing would only make her retreat.

Doris collected her thoughts and continued. "You see, if everyone just went on thinking Hank left and was only missing, I could never collect the insurance money. It wasn't a lot—and it wasn't the reason I kil…" She abruptly stopped talking and her hands fluttered bird-like from her lap to cover her mouth.

Goldstein's breath caught and he cocked his head sideways. His eyes widened slightly. To Doris he looked exactly like that dog in the old RCA Victor ads. *What was his name?* she wondered.

Oh, yeah, Nipper. Great, I am now confessing my crimes to a dog. This thought caused her to dissolve into shrill laughter again.

Goldstein struggled to maintain his composure and keep a neutral expression on his face. It wasn't easy. He had a lot more practice with the nice, pleasant "you can trust me, I'm a doctor" look. The "I just heard someone admit to murder" expression was going to take a little more time to master. It was a struggle to keep that doctorly countenance in place while trying to gauge the distance between himself and the door, and calculate exactly how long it would take to reach it. All at once the pretty lady before him became very scary. That single, tiny glimpse into the shadows behind her attractive façade sent chills down his spine.

Little by little Doris regained her composure and the feverish laughter quieted. Finally she shrugged. "Whoopsie. Guess I kinda let the cat out of the bag, didn't I?"

"You killed your first husband?"

Doris smiled disarmingly. "Guilty as charged."

Goldstein tried to speak and only a croak came out. He cleared his throat and tried again.

"You...you said it wasn't for the insurance money. Then why?"

Doris's eyes shot sideways. "There were lots of reasons; the drinking, the hitting, the women—all of it. One night I just snapped."

Goldstein could think of nothing to say. He was horrified to discover all his years of training had just abandoned him. The silence between them stretched out like an eternity.

Doris, feeling the awkwardness permeate the room like a draft, rushed on, "It's very important to me that you understand I am not a violent woman, Doctor. I am a good, god-fearing Christian, and really I would never hurt a fly. You believe that, don't you?"

Goldstein violently bobbed his head up and down.

"Good. Because I don't want you to think I'm some kind of black widow that goes around killing off my husbands. I adore Martin. He's a wonderful man and we are very happy. He's perfectly safe. Just so you know that. You do know that, right?" she begged emphatically.

Hearing the desperation in Doris Hughes's voice, Goldstein's training, as well as his survival instinct, both kicked back in at the same time. It was like someone had just pressed a reset button in his brain, turning off the temporary paralysis. He responded without hesitation, "Of course I do. Please, Mrs. Hughes, go on with your story."

Doris gave the doctor her best winning smile. "Maybe you should call me Doris now. Mrs. Hughes seems a little formal in light of what I just told you."

"Doris, then. Please go on." He began stroking his beard again in that irritatingly Freudian way.

Doris picked up her narrative from the night she murdered her husband. The story was a bit predictable, given what Dr. Goldstein had already learned of their relationship. Hank Sweeney had come home in his cups and flew into a rage when he discovered Doris had once again neglected to buy his whiskey. He went through at least five bottles a week, and it was hard for her to keep up with him. He had beaten her with his belt, forced himself on her sexually and then fallen asleep on top of her.

Violated, in pain, and weeping uncontrollably, Doris had wriggled out from beneath her husband's punishing weight and risen from the bed. Without thinking about what she was doing, she removed Hank's loaded gun from the nightstand. She did not hesitate as she put it to the back of her husband's head and pulled the trigger, silencing his loud snores once and for all.

She then lay down beside him and fell asleep amidst his blood and drying brain matter, until the first faint rays of daylight cut through the curtains of their bedroom.

It wasn't until then, she told Goldstein, that she could even think straight again.

"I knew I had to hide Hank and get the bedroom cleaned up. What I didn't realize, was just how hard it would be to move a dead body. Especially one that outweighed me by nearly a hundred pounds."

Goldstein felt vaguely nauseous. "So, what did you do?"

Her eyes took on a faraway look as she remembered. "I went to the garage and got Hank's moving dolly. I laid it on the floor and just sort of rolled him off the bed onto it. Then I covered him with a blanket and strapped him to the dolly with those bungee cord things. Somehow I got him out to the garage. I don't even remember doing it. I think it must have been like when you hear about those mothers who find the strength to lift cars off their babies. Adrenaline maybe?" she asked.

Goldstein shrugged. "So, what happened next?"

"We had a freezer in the garage. I took all the meat out and somehow maneuvered Hank inside. He was already getting stiff by then. I was so out of breath, I thought I was going to have a heart attack. I covered him with the meat and then just collapsed to the floor. I think I passed out for a few minutes."

Goldstein dreaded asking the next question. "How long did you leave him in the freezer?"

"For about two months."

Goldstein could feel acid churning in his stomach and bile coating his throat. He was beginning to lose the battle with his stomach. He offered Doris Hughes a beverage. She said she would take a Pepsi. He went to the small kitchen in the back of his office and removed two cans of soda from the fridge. He didn't like leaving her alone, where he couldn't keep an eye on her, but he knew if he didn't take a few moments away from her to regain his composure he was going to be sick. He held the cold can to his forehead for a moment.

Rearranging his face into his polite doctor expression was much harder this time, but he managed. Returning to the office, he handed Doris a soda.

"Thank you, Dr. Goldstein. Do you want to hear the rest? I think my hour was up a while ago. If you want I can get cash from the ATM to pay you for another hour. I didn't want to use Martin's insurance for the appointment, and I can't really write a check without him finding out. I don't want him to know I went to see a therapist."

"Don't worry about the money right now, Doris. I very much want to hear the rest. Does Martin know about any of your...ah...history?"

"Are you asking if he knows I killed Hank?"

Goldstein nodded. Just when he thought this couldn't get any weirder, she replied, "No. Martin is the detective who investigated his murder. I couldn't very well tell a policeman what I'd done, now could I?"

He looked at her incredulously. "Well, no. I guess you couldn't. Please go on."

"As I said, I left Hank in the freezer for two months. Then the dang nightmares started. I thought he was mad because it was probably pretty cold in there. I figured if I buried him proper, he'd go away and leave me alone once he thawed out. But there was no way I could move him by myself. So, I called Charmaine."

"This is your cousin, right?"

"Yeah, and she was my best friend in the whole world until...well never mind, I'll get to that later." Doris scowled and took a deep draught from the soda can. She stifled a burp behind one demurely raised hand, and said, "Excuse me."

"So did Charmaine help you move the body?" Goldstein asked like a child trying to rush a parent into finishing a much loved fairy tale. He was now completely sucked into this bizarre story and anxious to hear the rest.

"She did. I was afraid that she wouldn't, but she came through. Together we got Hank loaded into the trunk of her Buick. We buried him out in the woods late at night under a very nice tree. A Cottonwood, I think it was. I thought he would like it there. We also buried the mattress. There was no way that blood was going to come out. I flipped it over the night of Hank's little accident, but if anyone ever flipped it back...well, you know. There would be a lot of explaining to do. I painted the bedroom and then burned all the rags and sponges I had used to clean the mess after...afterward. The last piece of evidence I had to worry about was Hank's truck. If anyone saw it, they would know he hadn't left me for another woman. I rented a storage unit about fifty miles from town and kept it there. After we buried Hank, I took the blanket he had been wrapped in and put it with his truck."

"You certainly covered your tracks well," Goldstein said with real admiration.

"The tricky part came later, when I decided I wanted the insurance money. I needed everyone to start believing Hank was dead after all, but I didn't want them to find his body."

"You trusted Charmaine not to talk?"

Doris glowered and her hands balled into fists. "Oh, she had her own reasons for not telling. She was far more worried I would find out what she had done than she was about people learning of my misdeeds."

Goldstein was reminded that dear cousin Charmaine was now also deceased. He started to get a cold feeling in the pit of his stomach. "What was Charmaine so afraid you would discover?"

Tears filled Doris's eyes and she reached for a tissue on the table beside her. "I'm sorry, Doctor. Sixteen years later and this still hurts like hell."

Goldstein made some sympathetic noises and waited for Doris to go on. He was all but jumping out of his skin. He had to give the woman some credit. She had been smart enough to not only get away with murdering her husband, she even managed to get the detective who worked the case to fall in love with and marry her. That took some serious skills. Whether she was just extremely manipulative, or truly evil, Goldstein wasn't sure. He'd heard about plenty of women over the years in similar circumstances who killed abusive husbands. There was a network television series devoted to them, appropriately titled "Snapped." Most were usually caught or turned themselves in. There was always a battery of psychological experts, like himself for instance, who took the stand on their behalf during the trial. Some of these women were acquitted, but most spent the next decade or so behind bars.

Goldstein did not believe Doris was a threat to her current husband. What he would have to ponder was if she should pay for the murder of the last one, and if she was even sane enough to be left roaming freely in society. He would decide these things later. After the woman was safely out of his office and the door locked behind her. For now, he wanted to hear the second half of her narrative; the tale of Charmaine.

Doris dried her tears. "A few months after we buried Hank and I started thinking about the insurance, I took the truck out of storage. I parked it on a residential street just a few blocks from our house. I assumed someone would call it in if it stayed there long enough. I left the blanket inside the cab and the keys under the seat. I was careful to wipe my fingerprints from everything. I checked a few days later and the damn thing was still there. So, I placed an anonymous call to the police myself to report it. I knew it was risky, but I didn't want Hank's truck to just sit there until someone stole it. Then it might never be found and the world would just go on thinking the bastard left me. The truck was critical to making it look like he had met with foul play. With blood on the blanket inside, that would be the obvious conclusion, right?"

Goldstein agreed it would be.

"I acted surprised when the police showed up to tell me they had found Hank's truck, and even managed a few tears when they told me about the blanket. They changed it from a missing person's case to a homicide, and that's when I met Martin. He investigated me a little because I was the wife—who is always the first suspect, but I don't think he ever really thought I did it. At first he just felt sorry for me because of how Hank treated me. Then he felt even sorrier because I was a widow. Martin lost his wife a few years before. He was lonely and we became friends after the investigation was over. He helped me a lot with the insurance company by having Hank declared legally dead, even though they never found the body. Martin is a good man. My falling in love with him had nothing to do with what happened to Hank."

Goldstein didn't miss the tidy way Doris had of shifting the blame off of herself when she spoke of Hank's murder. She never said words like "after I killed him." It was always, "after what happened" or "Hank's little accident."

"So," Goldstein prompted, "about Charmaine?"

Doris's mouth puckered as though she had just tasted something foul. She inhaled a deep breath, as if she were about to embark on a laborious and much dreaded task, and said, "During the investigation Martin discovered Charmaine and Hank had been having an affair for years. Apparently, I was the only person in town who didn't know about it."

Goldstein nodded sympathetically. "And how did learning of their relationship after his death make you feel?"

Doris rolled her eyes. "How do you think it made me feel? I was completely devastated. When I asked Charmaine about it, she admitted it—didn't even try to lie. Just cried and begged my forgiveness. It was then that I understood what compelled her to help me when I needed to ah…relocate him. She felt guilty for betraying me."

The cold feeling in Goldstein's gut returned. "Doris, what did you do when you found out? Did you hurt her?"

In that moment, when Goldstein looked into Doris's eyes, he saw the horror-blackened madness she had so carefully hidden from the rest of the world churning just below the surface.

"What happened to Charmaine was an accident. Promise me you will remember that," she replied emphatically.

Goldstein swallowed hard. Suddenly all the spit in his mouth dried up. He reached absently for the Pepsi can beside him. "What happened to her, Doris?"

Doris sighed deeply and began picking at some imaginary lint on her slacks. She would no longer meet Goldstein's eyes.

"When I confronted Charmaine about the affair she got very upset. Kept telling me she never meant for it to happen. Like that was going to fix everything."

Doris pulled more tissue from the box and swiped violently at her eyes. Goldstein waited for her to continue. He was growing anxious once again, knowing how this tale would end.

"I couldn't stand the sight of her anymore, and just wanted to get away from her. I told her to get out of my house. She refused to leave and followed me up the stairs toward my bedroom. At the top of the staircase she grabbed my arm to restrain me, and when I tried to pull away she lost her balance and fell down the stairs." Doris finally raised her eyes and met Goldstein's incredulous stare.

She spat, "You don't believe me, do you? You think I pushed her." Her voice was accusatory.

Goldstein felt numb all over. He didn't trust himself to speak, but knew he must. "Of course I believe you, Doris. These things happen. Given the circumstances, I wonder how it is the police believed you though. Did you call them?"

In a wounded voice, Doris replied, "Of course I did! I called 911 immediately after Charmaine fell. And just so you know, her death was ruled an accident."

"Can I ask you something?"

"Sure."

"Was Martin the police officer assigned to the case?"

Doris smiled sweetly. "As a matter of fact, he was."

Goldstein wasn't surprised. He suspected the good detective had succumbed to Doris's charms from the first hello.

"Look, Doctor, I would be lying if I said I was sorry Charmaine was gone. After what she did behind my back with Hank she deserved what she got. Karma has a way of catching up with people, don't you think?"

Goldstein did not answer that question. "Getting back to the reason you came to see me. You said it was the nightmares about Hank and Charmaine?"

"Yes. I hope now that I have told someone the story they will go away and leave me alone. I've carried this around for sixteen long years without ever telling another living soul." Her eyes teared up again. "I can't get any rest, and to be honest, I am afraid I might say something in my sleep…something incriminating."

"Do you feel guilty for killing Hank?"

Doris considered the question before answering. "Not really. He was a lying and abusive bastard who was sleeping with my cousin. It's hard to feel too much guilt." She glanced at Goldstein briefly, "I'm sorry if you think that's cold."

"I only ask because I am trying to figure out why you have started dreaming about him again after all these years. Why now?"

"I don't know, Doctor. Maybe he and Charmaine got bored in Hell and decided to haunt me again."

"Do you really believe they are haunting you, or do you think these nightmares are a product of your own imagination?"

"I have no idea." Doris shrugged. "I'm just a flawed mortal fumbling my way toward enlightenment, right? You're the shrink, so you tell me."

Goldstein slipped back into his professional demeanor at last. Seeing his exit, he said, "Why don't we discuss that at our next session. Would you like to schedule another appointment?" He rose from his chair.

Doris told him she would need to think about it as she uncrossed her legs and smoothed her slacks. Rising from the chair, she asked, "You aren't going to tell anyone about our little chat today, are you, Doctor? Remember, you promised. You said only if I was a danger to anyone. Obviously, I am not."

Except me, Goldstein thought. He smiled reassuringly. "This was all a long time ago. I see no need to involve anyone else. I do hope that by telling me, you will be able to sleep better now, with no more bad dreams."

Doris reached out to shake his hand. "Thank you, Doctor. I'm sure I will. I feel ever so much better." She didn't fail to notice the Doctor's previously dry, firm handshake had turned cold and clammy.

With an enormous sigh of relief Goldstein ushered Doris outside and locked the door to the waiting room. He hurriedly closed the door to his office and locked that as well. It wasn't until he was barricaded in his office that the shakes came. He took a bottle of scotch from the drawer of his desk and pulled a long swig. He began to replace the bottle, and then took another. Wiping the back of his hand across his mouth, he drew a harsh and shuddering breath.

Once his nerves were sufficiently under control and the shuddering had subsided, he reached for the phone on his desk. He dialed Professor William O'Leary, his mentor and friend. Bill had been practicing psychiatry since the time Goldstein was still in Kindergarten.

After the pleasantries were exchanged, Goldstein said, "I need some professional advice."

"Sure, John. What's on your mind?" O'Leary asked.

"Suppose you had a patient who confessed to committing a crime over a decade ago. Would you go to the authorities?"

O'Leary was quiet for a minute as he contemplated the question. He asked, "How bad was the crime?"

"Bad."

O'Leary reminded Goldstein of the protocol all psychiatric professionals were supposed to follow when deciding to involve law enforcement. He told him that he would have to decide himself if this case warranted making such a call.

Goldstein thanked his friend for the advice, but when they hung up the phone he was no closer to knowing the right thing to do about Doris Hughes. He decided to go home and sleep on it. Though he normally never discussed his patients with his wife, he thought perhaps he would run this one by Pam. Maybe she could help him figure out if he should involve the police.

It was dark by the time Goldstein went to the parking lot to retrieve his car. He settled behind the wheel and was reaching for his seat belt when a gun was thrust against the back of his head. He uttered a startled squawk and reached for the door handle. The gun pressed harder against his skull, and soft lips grazed his left ear.

A gentle, feminine voice, tinged with deep regret, said, "Touch that door and I am going to kill you."

Goldstein stammered, "D…Doris is that you?"

Yeah, it's me, Doc." Doris sighed. "I'm really sorry about this, but I got to thinking about our talk. You really are the guy who knows too much. I suppose in hindsight I shouldn't have uh…shared so much. But, it's a little too late for me to take it back now, and I am fresh out of magic wands."

"Doris, listen to me. I am not going to tell anyone about what you did. You can trust me. I just want to help you."

"I know that. The problem is, you are one of those guys who always tries to do the right thing. I could see that right away. I'm married to a fellow just like you. Eventually you would be tortured by the knowledge of what I did. The weight of it all would just become too much and you would have to report it. If you are honest with yourself, you will know I'm right about this."

Goldstein, visibly trembling, began vehemently protesting. Doris silenced his protests the same hideous way she had silenced her first husband's snores. As she exited the car, she spared the doctor's lifeless body a final glance. "Sorry, Doc," she said, as her heels echoed down the parking lot.

Doris Hughes kissed her husband goodnight. She was confident there would be no nocturnal visits from Hank tonight. She had unburdened herself, and everyone knows confession is good for the soul. While she was sorry the doctor had become collateral damage, she was sure she had solved the problem.

Three hours later, Doris awoke and stuffed the pretty purple comforter against her lips to stifle the scream trying to escape her burning throat. Her breath was coming in short little gasps and a thin sheen of sweat had broken out on her arms and between her breasts. More sweat pooled against the small of her back. Her hair felt greasy against her neck, and her damp nightgown clung like a cobweb.

The image of Hank's brittle bones struggling to rise against the tangled tree roots that had become like twisting serpents in his final resting place was just beginning to fade. They had grown over and between his bones, into the moldering mattress beneath him. It was as though the roots were in an eternal struggle to hold him down and prevent him from rising and pursuing Doris.

Charmaine was even worse, with her staring, lifeless eyes, the drying blood, and that telltale dent in the side of her skull; the wound that screamed the truth. It was no fall that killed Charmaine. It was a tire iron brandished by a woman scorned and hell-bent on revenge. Martin had closed the case awfully quickly. She wondered if he ever suspected.

Doris glanced at the other side of the bed and was relieved to see her husband sleeping soundly. She had not woken him.

Why wouldn't they stay dead? Hank and Charmaine were still tormenting her. And this time they weren't alone. They had brought Doctor Goldstein with them. He was stroking that ridiculous beard, with blood still pouring down his neck and the smoking hole from the .32 gaping behind his ear like an opening into the very pits of Hell. Why wouldn't they all just leave her alone?

Perhaps, Doris thought, *it has to be an actual priest in order for confession to work. Yes! That must be it. Tomorrow I will call Father Sullivan. He can absolve me with a hundred Hail Mary's or something. I do hope he has the good sense not to report me. I would so miss his sermons...*

AS THE CROW FLIES

AFTER A FUTILE battle to hang onto her house amid a messy and bitter divorce, Brianna Douglas accepted the inevitable and allowed her wretched ex-husband to sell the marital residence and cash her out for her half.

After eight years of feeding the neighborhood birds and squirrels she hoped they would be able to adjust to the lack of birdseed, shelled peanuts and grain bread she left out for them on a daily basis. Her mother assured her that animals were very adaptable and they would make do without her. Brianna hoped that was true. She had offered to leave both the birdbath and feeder for the new owners, but they did not want them. Brianna couldn't help feeling guilty, as though she was letting the neighborhood wildlife down.

As is usually the case when a couple gets divorced, their friends picked a side. Few landed in Brianna's camp. It was understandable. Rob, her ex, had a mini-mansion boasting a movie theatre with surround-sound, and an Olympic size swimming pool complete with a skinny, topless supermodel named Ariel.

The only thing Rob hadn't fought for in the divorce was their cat, Bartholomew. Ariel was allergic to cats.

Brianna came from humbler means and returned to them after she and Rob broke up. During the eight years she was married she enjoyed the lavish lifestyle his income as a neurosurgeon provided, but once the divorce was final, she was just as happy to trade in the Mercedes she was awarded in the divorce for a nice sensible Subaru. She hadn't married Rob for his money, and only quit her job at his request when they were married. He wanted a stay-at-home domestic goddess, and that is just what Brianna had been for the duration of her married life.

The first year and a half or so was good. After that it was five years of contentious arguments, numerous other women, and one embarrassing sexually transmitted disease Rob brought home and never told her about. She had to find out she had contracted it the hard way—by experiencing the entire gamut of appalling symptoms. It was the chlamydia that finally drove Brianna to take the cat and leave.

After a hellish year of attorneys, unreasonable settlement demands, and Rob's frantic attempt to transfer all his holdings to off-shore bank accounts before the judge froze his assets, the divorce was at last final. The courts were generous and Brianna was awarded a healthy settlement, including a very comfortable monthly alimony.

Later in the day, after the judgment had been rendered, Rob left a scathing and profane message on Brianna's voicemail. He claimed the judge who presided over their divorce was a lesbian, and implied that Her Honor and Brianna were involved in a sordid relationship—the details of which, he described in most colorful and graphic terms. Numerous and increasingly threatening messages punctuated the next three months of Brianna's life, until her lawyer filed a restraining order to force Rob to stop calling.

It came as little surprise when after only six months Rob took her back to court to have the alimony reduced. He had yet to send her one check on time, and two months he never sent it at all.

Rob lost this battle, prompting another round of vicious and screaming phone messages, followed by an injunction leveled against him and a steep fine imposed by the judge. Brianna had a very good lawyer.

While she left the marriage far from poor, Brianna could not afford, nor did she desire, another huge house in a pretentious neighborhood. She settled for a comfortable three-year-old Colonial in a nice, well-maintained community on the other side of town. She bought the house because of the beautifully manicured and fenced backyard. It had mature trees, lush foliage and a covered patio suitable for her favorite pastime—bird watching. An amateur ornithologist, Brianna came to love all the different species who visited the feeder in her old home. She was anxious to make the acquaintance of the birds in her new neighborhood.

Upon getting settled, the first thing Brianna did was set up the bird feeder and begin a morning ritual of toasting grain bread and scattering it on the lawn in her backyard.

Within a week, three crows began waiting each morning for Brianna to arrive with the toast. She would enjoy her coffee on the patio while the crows came to nibble on the bread. She spoke to them, and they cawed conversation in return.

After two weeks of settling into this routine, Brianna was surprised to find a small and very pretty Abalone shell on the edge of her patio one morning. She knew at once that the crows had left it for her. When she picked it up, she saw one of the crows watching her intently from the top of the fence. "Did you give this to me?" she asked him.

The crow cawed once and bobbed its head.

Wow, thought Brianna. It was almost as though he understood what she asked and had nodded in the affirmative.

"Well, thank you. It's lovely."

Not long after that, about once a week Brianna would receive a small gift or trinket on her patio from the crows. There was a broken bit of stained glass once, a few coins, a couple seashells, and once an actual gold ring with a jade colored stone that was quite beautiful. The birds seemed to like shiny objects, and from Brianna's point of view they had pretty good taste. She put the stained glass piece up in the garden window in her kitchen. Everything else she saved in a keepsake box she bought just for the gifts the crows bestowed upon her.

As the season changed and the weather grew warmer, Brianna took up jogging. She became friendly with a few people who lived on her block. She got to know Bobby and Renee Christopher, the couple who lived next door. They always complimented Brianna on how beautiful her garden was. They noticed the numerous birds always visiting Brianna's feeder or perched in the trees in her yard.

Brianna liked the couple, and one day invited Renee over for a glass of wine in the late afternoon.

As the two women sat chatting on Brianna's patio, a large flock of birds twittered loudly and rose up en-masse from a pine tree at the back of Brianna's yard. They fluttered off into the horizon.

Renee gasped and put a hand to her chest. "Good lord, that was like a scene right out that Hitchcock movie. Don't all those birds creep you out just a little?"

Brianna was taken aback by the question. "No, not at all. I love the birds. Especially my crows. I have three that come for breakfast every morning."

Renee Christopher wrinkled her nose. "Ew! Crows? They are such nasty things. Aren't they supposed to be a bad omen or something?"

To bring the point home she raised a gold cross she wore around her neck and held it up, as if to ward off the evil birds.

Brianna, sounding slightly amused, replied, "I believe you have them confused with vampires. They are actually incredibly smart birds."

"Well, I don't like them. As long as they stay on your side of the fence." Renee laughed uncomfortably and drained her wine glass.

As Renee rose to leave, Brianna was startled to see two of the crows perched in her pink Dogwood tree watching her neighbor with bright-eyed interest. They did not shift their gaze until the woman had disappeared inside her back door.

Brianna asked, "Did you guys hear that? Don't worry about it. Your breed just has a bad rap, that's all. Want some peanuts, guys?" She shook some from a bag onto the lawn before going inside.

Three days later Brianna found a present at the edge of her patio. It was a gold necklace that looked suspiciously like the cross Renee Christopher had been wearing.

Brianna picked it up and bounced it on her palm. *No, it can't be,* she thought. She looked around her yard, but the crows were nowhere to be seen. She carried the cross inside and placed it in the keepsake box.

The following week as she was just leaving for her run, Renee flagged her down. Brianna stopped to see what her neighbor wanted. She was only a little surprised when Renee asked, "You haven't seen a gold cross lying around anywhere have you? I lost mine."

Brianna told her she hadn't, but that she would keep an eye out for it when she was out jogging. She pondered the situation. She knew crows were smart, but were they really smart enough to over-hear a conversation and get offended enough to steal someone's jewelry? She didn't think so. Brianna reasoned that it had to be a coincidence. Renee must have dropped the necklace outside somewhere and one of the crows found it. They left it for Brianna, just as they had the other items frequently placed on the patio for her. While the cross wasn't as sparkly as most of the items the crows seemed to favor, this was not the first piece of jewelry to show up on her patio.

Brianna waited a couple of days before placing the cross on Renee's front porch in a conspicuous location where she knew it would be found.

That same morning, while the crows nibbled at the toast she put out, she told them, "Hey, don't steal the neighbor's stuff anymore. Even if you don't like her. Capiche?"

Having lost his last attempt at having Brianna's alimony lowered, Rob tried again six months later. Frustrated and still paying off the legal fees from her divorce, Brianna sat on her patio in tears reading the court summons. She explained the situation to her sister on the phone and wept bitterly about having to endure another costly legal battle with her greedy ex-husband. Sometimes it seemed like this nightmare would never end.

After hanging up the phone with her sister, Brianna watched the crows as they picked at the bread. She asked, "How do you guys do it? How do you mate for life? We humans try, but I married a bastard who I feel like I will be fighting with for the rest of my life. Damn Rob Douglas and his anorexic super-model, too," she spat, slamming her hand down hard enough on the patio table to startle two chickadees into flight from the birdfeeder.

The largest of the three crows paused with a piece of toast in his mouth. With his head titled sideways, he looked curiously at

Brianna for a long moment before cawing to his mates and returning his attention to the bread.

A few days later when Brianna went out to fill the birdfeeder she noticed something odd. There was a pattering of red dots splashed across her patio and an item that she could not immediately identify lying where the crows always left her presents.

After filling the feeder with birdseed, Brianna knelt down to examine what the crows had brought her. It was lacking the usual shiny hue of most of their offerings, and for the first few seconds Brianna could not comprehend what she was seeing.

When she recognized it for what it was, Brianna gasped and shot to her feet. All of a sudden the red dots spattered across her patio made a very sick kind of sense. She backed away from the object and looked around for the crows. They were nowhere to be seen.

With a queasy stomach, Brianna went inside for a roll of paper towels. She wasn't going to touch what she had just found with her bare hands.

Donning kitchen gloves, she gingerly rolled it onto a paper towel and disposed of it in the waste can kept by the side of the house.

The crows had left her a human finger.

Brianna went inside and washed her hands. She shuddered, wondering if someone wasn't looking for the thing, wanting to reattach it to the hand from which it had been severed. She wondered where the crows could have possibly found such a bizarre entity. She assumed the digit must have been separated by some type of tractor or industrial accident in a field or on a farm somewhere. She knew these things happened occasionally. Brianna had once dated a man whose mother mowed off three of her toes with a power lawnmower many years ago. Of course, this happened in the backwoods of Arkansas. Brianna rather doubted that type of thing happened very often here in the suburbs of Southern California.

The question was: Why would the crows think a severed finger would make a nice gift for her? How did they graduate from sparkly seashells and odd bits of jewelry to this?

Okay, she thought. *Now it's creepy.*

Later that day, she rented a pressure washer and set to work cleaning the blood spatter from her patio. As she fired up the washer the crows watched and cawed at her from the Dogwood. In a hushed tone she muttered, "Don't bring me anymore body parts, okay birdies?"

After removing the blood, she went inside and carried Bartholomew away from the window where he always sat to watch the birds in the yard, while making what she called his bird-voice— a strange clicking sound that was nothing at all like his normal meow. She closed the curtains, cutting off both of their views of the yard. She didn't feel like looking at the birds—and especially the crows today. She was having a little too much trouble digesting the nasty surprise they had left her.

Two months later, Brianna returned to court for the hearing on the reduction of her alimony. She felt a strange sense of déjà vu as she looked around the dismal courtroom. The entire experience was like visiting a movie set. Nothing had changed since the last time she was here, not even the players.

There was the painfully thin model; sitting behind Rob and constantly rubbing his shoulders and cooing in his ear, while simultaneously staring daggers at Brianna. And of course, her ex-husband; looking in ill-temper as he conferred with his counsel and absentmindedly batted the model's hand away. There was Rob's lawyer, Mr. Silverstein; looking through documents and whispering in his client's ear. And her own attorney, Paula; chewing on the end of a ballpoint pen and reviewing her notes.

Brianna did her best to ignore her ex. There were two attorneys between them—Rob's, extremely overweight, and blocking the view of her ex-husband quite nicely. She reminded herself that this would all be over soon, and she wouldn't have to come back to this miserable place again until Rob threw his next tantrum about the alimony. Paula had assured her the chances of the judge granting Rob's motion to have her support reduced were extremely unlikely.

The court was called to order and Rob's attorney rose to make his argument to the judge.

"Your Honor, my client has suffered a debilitating injury that has impacted his ability to perform his job. It will substantially decrease his earning capability for the foreseeable future. In light of this new circumstance, we must respectfully request that you grant our motion for a reduction in the amount of alimony Doctor Douglas pays, to an amount that will commensurate with his reduced income."

The judge replied, "I see. And exactly what is this debilitating injury your client has suffered, counselor?"

The attorney raised Rob's arm and showed the judge. "You see, Your Honor? The poor man has lost a finger on his left hand. It's been devastating for him."

Brianna's breath caught. All at once her heart began fluttering like the wings of the birds she loved so much. She was overcome by a jolting sense of vertigo and grasped the edge of the table to keep from listing sideways.

Her attorney, hearing Brianna's sharp intake of breath, placed her hand over her client's and patted it reassuringly. Paula whispered, "Stay cool, Bri."

The judge asked, "May I see the documentation which supports your claim of Doctor Douglas's reduced earnings please? I assume you have written confirmation from the treating physician that states he is no longer able to perform surgery."

The lawyer stumbled. "Err..well, Your Honor, I did not say my client was unable to operate on his patients. He can still do that, but he won't be performing nearly as many of these procedures as he did before he sustained such an egregious injury. Therefore, it stands to reason that his earnings will decrease."

Paula rose from the defense table, "Your Honor, we object to any change in alimony based on Doctor Douglas's assumption that his future earnings will be affected by his injury. Without proof that he is making less money at this time, we strongly object to this motion. While we are sorry for Doctor Douglas's unfortunate wound, I would like to note that he is right handed, and the loss sustained was to his left. We believe this is nothing more than yet another attempt by the plaintiff to try and get out of his obligation to provide spousal support for Mrs. Douglas."

The judge smiled at Paula, and said, "I've got this, counselor. Objection noted."

Turning back to Rob's lawyer, she asked, "Mr. Silverstein, have you any documentation to show the court that substantiates your claim? Even Doctor Douglas's last paycheck stub will suffice. If his income has declined, it will be reflected there."

"Your Honor, I think the fact that he will be making less money should be obvious! He's a surgeon who is now handicapped! From which hand the finger is missing is completely irrelevant."

"So, I take it your answer is no? There is no proof. Is that correct?"

The lawyer bellowed, "The proof is the man's horribly disfigured hand! You can clearly see that his finger is missing, can't you? What other proof do you need, Judge?"

The judge's sunny disposition disappeared instantly. Her mouth thinned to a severe line.

"You will want to watch your tone, counselor. You are just one outburst shy of sanctions."

Silverstein hastily apologized and returned to his seat.

The judge glared at Rob. "Doctor Douglas, it is this court's understanding that you have been consistently late in paying the previously ordered payments due your ex-wife. I am putting you on notice that going forward I am imposing interest compounded daily in the amount of twenty percent for each day Mrs. Douglas's alimony check is late. Furthermore, while I sympathize with your injury, it is no excuse for your repeated waste of this court's time with these frivolous and groundless motions. I don't want to see you in my courtroom again unless you have, not only a valid reason to ask for a reduction in spousal support, but the physical documentation to back up such a request. Your ex-wife's countersuit requesting you pay the attorney fees she incurred to fight this proceeding is hereby granted. Your motion for reduction in alimony is denied. Court is adjourned."

Brianna had to know how Rob lost his finger. It was one thing to say the neighbor's necklace showing up was a coincidence. It was entirely another to assume the gruesome finger presented by the crows wasn't Rob's.

Not one given to superstition, Brianna refused to believe that somehow the crows knew of her trouble with her ex-husband and decided to take matters into their own beaks. The whole notion that the crows she fed every morning could have possibly done something like this was ludicrous.

One of the few couples who Brianna was still on friendly terms with from her married life was Larry and Sue Conner. She called Sue on a fishing expedition to find out how Rob had come up one finger short. She prayed there was some reasonable explanation waiting at the other end of the phone line.

After the pleasantries were exchanged, Brianna did not even have to ask Sue what happened. Her friend brought it up first. She asked, "Bri, did you hear what happened to Rob?"

Acting like she had no idea what Sue was talking about, Brianna responded, "No, what?"

"It was really weird. He got his finger bitten off, if you can believe that."

"Really? How did that happen?" Brianna closed her eyes waiting for Sue's response.

"Larry said something about a flock of crows attacking him while he was asleep on a lounge chair by the pool."

Brianna bit her lip. "A murder," she muttered.

"Huh?" Sue asked.

"A group of crows is called a murder, not a flock."

Sue said, "Okay, well, they murdered the ring finger on Rob's left hand." And then she giggled at her own joke.

Brianna was silent for so long, Sue asked, "Hello, Bri? Are you still there?"

"Crows, you say? How many were there?"

"I think Larry said three. Pretty crazy, huh? Maybe it was revenge of the birds. You always liked the feathered critters so much. Kind of ironic it was his wedding ring finger." Once again, Sue laughed.

When she realized Brianna wasn't laughing with her, she quickly added, "Sorry, guess that probably wasn't funny."

Brianna hurried off the phone. She dissolved into hysterical laughter that gradually turned to sobs. Once she finally had herself under control, she wiped her eyes, drank a cool draught of water and headed to the patio to have a never-imagined conversation with her crows.

Brianna looked at the Dogwood, one of the crows' favorite perches, and did not see them there. Nor were they on the fence or anywhere else visible in the yard. She peeked over the fence to make sure no one was in the neighbor's yard. This was one chat she would never want over-heard.

Brianna began cautiously, "Hey there, crows. You guys out here? We need to have a little talk, you and I." Then she dissolved into giggles again that threatened to turn right back into hysteria.

Brianna drew in a couple of deep breaths to quell the laughter bubbling up and trying desperately to overtake her. The situation was just so uncanny she couldn't even believe it was happening. She went inside and splashed cool water on her face. She drank a shot of bourbon then headed back outside.

"Okay, crows, now listen up because I only plan on saying this once. If you lobbed off my ex-husband's finger, I am forbidding you from ever doing anything like that again...unless of course next time you want to bite off his...well never mind." That did it.

Krystal Lawrence

Brianna came utterly unglued. She laughed so hard tears were streaming from her eyes and she couldn't catch her breath. She grew lightheaded and was forced to put her head between her knees to keep from passing out. It would take several minutes before she could regain her composure enough to continue this monologue.

When she began speaking again she heard a single caw in return. All at once the trio of crows landed in a line on the grass a few feet from where she sat.

Though her heartbeat sped up a little, she managed to keep the hysteria at bay this time. Having no prior experience calling off attack crows who were working on her behalf, the words did not come easily.

It was disconcerting looking at the three pair of black eyes trained intently on her face. Rising, Brianna said, "Hold that thought," and escaped back inside the house. She returned a moment later with the bottle of bourbon clutched in her hand.

Taking a long swig directly from the bottle, Brianna looked into each crow's eyes. She cautiously began again, "It seems like maybe you guys understand what I am saying when I talk to you. I still have a hard time believing you attacked Rob, but there certainly is evidence to support that theory. So that's why I am giving it to you straight here. For all I know all three of you are Rhode's Scholars and speak the Queen's English."

Brianna held up a hand, as though the bird's had just disagreed with her. She took another drink from the bottle of bourbon. "If that's true, please do me a favor and don't start talking now. I am freaked out enough without having to listen to you recite Shakespeare or something."

In the middle of this monologue Brianna's phone rang. She looked down at the caller ID and groaned. It was Rob. Obviously

54

furious with the judge for the beating he took in court today, he was calling to take his frustration out on Brianna again.

Under normal circumstances Brianna would have let it go to voicemail and then sicked Paula on him. But emboldened by the whiskey, she answered the call.

She got as far as listening to him thunder, "You ball breaking bitch!" before holding the phone away from her ear for the rest of his tirade.

Hearing Rob's voice roaring through the phone, the crows went crazy. They began agitatedly cawing and flying in circles around the yard. Startled by their violent reaction, Brianna jumped up from the table, knocking the bourbon bottle over and sending it crashing to the patio. Brianna watched in dismay as amber colored liquid ran in all directions. When she glanced back up, she was shocked to see all three crows had flown onto the patio and were diving directly at her.

Brianna uttered a startled squawk and dropped the phone. She ran into the house and slammed the back door behind her. As she looked through the glass, she watched in awe as the birds furiously attacked the phone. They began violently pecking at it and scrambled to keep purchase with their claws. Brianna could not believe her eyes, as bits of plastic began flying from the phone trapped between them. Screeching loud and angry caws, they carried it off the patio. Both the phone and the crows disappeared into the foliage in a cloud of dust.

Shaken, Brianna cautiously opened the back door when the frenzy had passed. She stepped out onto the patio. If the crows showed any sign of aggression toward her she would flee right back indoors to safety. She didn't think she was in any danger, however. She realized it wasn't herself who their anger was directed at. It was Rob.

"Hey, guys. Where are you?" Brianna called toward the yard.

The bushes shook and the largest of the three crows emerged. He voiced one soft caw and then flew up and out of the yard. A moment later his two companions followed suit and flew away.

Brianna knelt down and felt around underneath the bush where they had disappeared with the phone. Finding it, she assessed the damage. The case was splintered, with a zigzagging crack running right down the center. Though the screen was deeply gouged and covered in scratches, surprisingly, the phone was still operational. She dusted it off on her jeans and went back inside the house.

Rob called three more times. Brianna let the calls go to voicemail. She would call Paula in the morning and let her know the harassment had started up again. In the meantime, she had more important things to think about. Like what to do about the crows. She was starting to worry they might decide to attack Rob again.

The following morning when she went outside with the toast for them, there was a scatter of wildflowers in the place on her patio where the crows always left their gifts. She wondered if this wasn't their way of apologizing for yesterday's outburst. They were certainly remarkable birds. Frightening, but remarkable.

As she tossed the bread onto the lawn the crows flew into the yard and landed on the grass. They looked at Brianna before approaching the toast she had put out.

"Well, go on. Eat your breakfast. I'm not mad at you if that's what you are afraid of, but you have to leave Rob alone. As I recall from Sunday school, the bible says nothing about vengeance is mine sayeth the crows."

As they ate the bread the black birds did not spare Brianna another glance. Appearing completely uninterested in what she was saying, they finished the bread and flew off into the mild morning breeze.

Over the next few days everything seemed to return to normal. The morning routine continued, with the crows waiting for their breakfast and cawing good-naturedly. No gifts of dubious origin were left for Brianna on the patio. In fact, they left nothing for her at all. She hoped the crisis was over and the birds would not bother Rob again.

She could no longer convince herself that her crows were not responsible for maiming his hand. She understood that they had become fiercely loyal to her. What she could not figure out was how they knew where to find her ex-husband. These were no ordinary birds. While Brianna had never believed much in supernatural phenomenon, she recognized something of that nature was at work here. She couldn't afford the luxury of ignoring it anymore. However, there really was nothing she could do about the situation. It certainly appeared the crows were on her side. She didn't believe they would harm her. While she would remain vigilant to their behavior, she could not force them to stay away from Rob. All she could do was tell them to leave him alone and hope they would obey her request.

What was now of greater worry was Rob himself. His behavior since losing the fight to have Brianna's alimony cut had become increasingly violent and erratic.

Brianna didn't know what to worry about more; Rob harming her, or the crows harming him.

The escalation began with Paula calling Rob's lawyer and telling him to rein in his client. If the scathing phone messages continued, she told Silverstein she would file for another injunction. Rob ignored the warning and was leveled with another hefty fine.

That only made matters worse. The calls increased in volume and severity. In desperation, Brianna changed her phone number.

This so incensed Rob, he began nearly nightly visits to Brianna's house. In a drunken rage, he would bang on the front door, hurling offensive insults and calling her filthy names. He demanded she "stop robbing him blind."

Another restraining order was filed. It did nothing to dissuade him.

Finally, out of his mind with fury from Brianna's refusal to open the door to his maniacal ravings, Rob stumbled to his car, shouting threats over his shoulder. Intending to roar from the house with tires squealing, he slammed his Porsche into the wrong gear and floored it. Sailing over the curb into Bobby and Renee's front yard, he took out their mailbox and several flower beds, before plowing into their garage door and causing himself a mild concussion when the airbag deployed.

The police and paramedics were called. After spending three hours in the emergency room, Rob was charged with destruction of property, violating a restraining order and driving while under the influence. He spent two nights in county lock-up, until Ariel could arrange to make bail.

Brianna did not know if it was the head injury, or the time in jail and the battery of legal problems he was now facing, but something seemed to have done the trick. For two blissful weeks Rob left Brianna completely alone.

She gradually began to get her nerves back under control and stop bracing for the sound of his pummeling fists and vulgar obscenities booming outside her front door every night. Her neighbor's garage and the damage to their property was covered by Rob's insurance. Fortunately they did not blame Brianna for her ex-husband's conduct.

She could not believe Rob had gone so completely crazy. While she always knew that money was his god, Brianna never dreamed he was capable of such out of control behavior. After all, he had a reputation to uphold as a respected surgeon. The court of public opinion always mattered so much to him in the past. She wondered if he knew he was putting his whole life in jeopardy by behaving so recklessly.

She didn't even want to think about what the crows were capable of if they got wind of Rob's misdeeds. Fortunately all of his dangerous pursuits had taken place late at night when they were in their nest asleep. Brianna realized she did not even know where the crows' nest was located. For all she knew they lived in one of the tall trees in her backyard. That thought caused a nasty shiver of fright to crawl up her spine. What if all the commotion had woken them, and they were even now planning retribution? She never dreamed life could become so insane.

A short time later, time would prove Brianna had no idea what true insanity really looked like. She found out not too long after convincing herself that both her ex-husband and the crows were done causing her any grief.

On an overcast Tuesday, Brianna awoke to a commotion out on her back patio in the early morning hours. Glancing at the clock next to her bed, she saw it was just after sunrise.

Having no idea what all the racket was, Brianna flung open the window shade in her bedroom. Taking in the unbelievable scene playing out below her in the backyard, she stumbled away from the window and screamed.

Literally hundreds of birds were whirling in a dizzying cloud on her lawn. They formed a tight sphere and appeared to be pecking and clawing at something caught between them. Brianna had never seen so many birds at once.

The way they were moving together in that frenzied dance was worse than anything from even Tippi Hedren's worst nightmare.

All were converging on an unknown victim, in a blinding array of colors, shapes and sizes. Brianna could not see where one bird ended and another began. Their claws were working, their beaks snapping, and God help whatever was caught in the middle of the murderous orb they had formed.

She ran from the bedroom, taking the stairs two at a time. As she approached the back door she heard the mad cacophony of thousands of beating wings. Bartholomew hissed and charged between Brianna's feet and up the stairs, retreating to the safety of her bedroom.

Brianna cautiously opened the curtains on the back door. She watched in dumbstruck horror as the colorful shroud of madly pecking birds elevated into the sky. It was impossible to see if her trio of crows was a part of that insane roaring tapestry.

Brianna collapsed against the door as the thick veil of screaming feathers flew over the house and due south. Just as they were ascending over the trees, Brianna uttered an anguished moan.

Peeking from between all those madly rushing bodies was Rob's staring face. It was frozen in a death mask and covered in dozens of bleeding scratches. Where his right eye should have been was only a bloody gaping hole. She saw this grisly scene for only a few seconds before the birds disappeared over the horizon.

With shaking hands Brianna unlocked the back door and stepped out onto her patio. Apart from several brightly colored feathers lying on the patio and strewn about the yard, there remained no evidence of the unspeakable horror she had just witnessed.

She plucked a single sleek black feather from the Dogwood tree and staggered back onto the patio. Falling into a chair, she called weakly, "Hey, crows. Are you guys here?"

The morning remained eerily still, and silent as a tomb. Her feeder sat empty and there was nothing perched in any of the bushes or trees. For the first time since she moved in there was not a single bird anywhere in Brianna Douglas's yard.

Eyes glazed over in shock, Brianna sat slumped against the table for several minutes. When the doorbell rang she recoiled as though a canon had been fired next to her head.

Sucking in harsh gasps of air, she rose on wobbly legs and made her way to the front door. She did not recognize her visitors, but began shaking uncontrollably when she saw a police car parked in her driveway.

Convinced Rob's body had already been found, she was sure the men on her porch were there to arrest her. She was the only person alive with a motive to kill him. It would, of course, be futile to try and explain to the authorities what fate had actually befallen him. Who in their right mind would believe it? She barely believed it herself. Brianna hoped Paula knew a good criminal defense attorney.

Neither of the two men waiting at her front door wore a police uniform. They were in business suits. Brianna steeled herself for their accusations and opened the door.

They smiled politely and held up their badges for her inspection. "Mrs. Douglas?"

Unable to trust herself to speak, Brianna nodded.

"I am Detective Ramirez, and this is my partner Detective Soames. We are sorry to disturb you at this hour, but we have reason to believe your life may be in danger."

This was not what she was expecting to hear. For several seconds she did nothing but look back and forth between the two men, her brow knitted in confusion. Finally, Brianna whispered, "What?"

"Ma'am, we received a phone call this morning from a woman named Ariel Forbes. She claimed that her boyfriend—your ex-husband, Robert Douglas, was on his way over to your house with a gun. According to Ms. Forbes, he was planning to kill you. We put out an APB on his vehicle and it was located about a block from here. We were afraid we might have been too late. Have you seen or heard from Mr. Douglas today?"

Brianna shook her head. Tears welled in her eyes and she sagged against the door frame. The detective who had done all the talking put a supportive arm around her waist.

He said sympathetically, "I know this is a lot to absorb. May we come in? We don't want to leave you alone until Mr. Douglas is apprehended. There are officers and a canine unit in the area looking for him. It's only a matter of time before we catch him."

Brianna allowed the officers inside. She looked nervously toward the backyard and was relieved to see all was quiet there.

Brianna offered the detectives coffee, but her hands were shaking so badly she spilled the grounds all over the floor. Detective Soames wiped them up while Ramirez got the coffee pot going. Brianna excused herself to get dressed and went upstairs to her bedroom.

The full impact of what the detectives had told her hit her like a ton of bricks and she collapsed onto the bed. She now understood what this morning's hellish occurrence was all about. The birds had saved her life. Equally amazing; the skinny, anorexic bitch alerted the cops to Rob's plans in an effort to spare Brianna from his wrath. She supposed she should thank her.

Robert Douglas's body was never found. His disappearance was investigated and even made news headlines. The case was listed as unsolved in the police archives. His fate remained a mystery to everyone. Only Brianna knew the truth.

Eventually the birds returned to her yard—all except the crows. Brianna waited for them every morning and left toast for them on the grass, but they did not show up.

After several months, Brianna accepted that they probably weren't coming back. She missed them a great deal.

She reasoned they had been her guardian angels, and once they saved her from Rob, their job was done.

It was a pleasant surprise when the following summer she found a sparkling seashell waiting for her at the edge of the patio one morning.

She shaded her eyes against the sun and peered up into the Dogwood. The crows weren't there.

That was okay. She smiled and held up the shell anyway. "Thanks, this is very pretty. Come back and see me, okay? I miss you guys."

The next morning Brianna awoke to the familiar sound of the crows cawing, and looked out the window to see all three of them waiting patiently for their toast on the lawn.

THE ETERNAL SHERIFF

PART ONE

GRANT HUDSON KNEW the town of Sidewinder, South Dakota better than anyone else. He was on a first name basis with the Sheriff, Wayne Dearborn, and his faithful sidekick, Deputy John Starr. He knew the saloon girls, Kitten and Miss Dolly, and was pretty chummy with Paddy the cook and the bartender Earl, too. He was even quite close to the outlaw, Mad-Dog Pete, and the stagecoach robbers who called themselves the Midnight Riders.

Grant was the person who created the town of Sidewinder and all its residents, and for the past seven years they had provided him with a very nice life.

While he would never be Louis L'Amour, Grant had a strong following of dedicated readers who purchased his books faithfully, and a publishing contract with one of the better houses. He also had one hell of a drinking problem.

On his third marriage—the one he really hoped would stick— and not just because of how expensive the last two divorces were, but because he genuinely loved Margie, Grant did his drinking at the country club rather than at home.

They had a nice house with a view of the fairway in the exclusive golf club community of Gatesville, and the clubhouse was just around the corner from their house. After getting pulled over and narrowly talking his way out of a DUI arrest the previous month, Grant took to drinking within walking distance of his home. After all, what would Sheriff Dearborn have to say about a man who drove all liquored-up like that? He definitely would not approve.

The clubhouse bartender often stayed after closing to accommodate Mr. Hudson's thirst.

Grant began to realize his drinking was getting out of hand right around the same time he decided it was time to kill off Sheriff Dearborn in the Sidewinder series, and pin the badge to the breast of Deputy Starr. Dearborn had been the sheriff since the first book in the series, *Lights Out Over Sidewinder*, and it was time to shake things up.

It was easy to put the drinking issue on the back burner when you had more pressing things on your mind—such as a deadline, and a book that was neither finished, nor in the capable hands of Marta the editor, where it was supposed to be.

This was the first time since signing that very lucrative contract with the publishing house that Grant had ever skated this close to a deadline, and it was not good. The morning he awoke to a somewhat terse email from Emery Cleary, his publisher, Grant figured he better cut back on the booze and get working on Sheriff Dearborn's sad ending. He missed the folks in Sidewinder anyway. He sure hadn't been visiting as often as he should have been lately.

Grant was not convinced too much scotch was entirely to blame either. He was pretty sure that somewhere in his subconscious he was just very reluctant to write the ending to the good sheriff's life. A guy gets attached to the characters he creates after so many years, and fictional or not, an author always grieves the death of one of his favorites—even when he knows the time has come.

Grant had transformed the lanai at the back of the house into his office. It was glass-walled on three sides and had a sweeping view of the green and the ninth hole of the Gatesville Golf Course. Just beyond his office was a patio where his wife kept an herb garden.

With the deadline barreling down on Grant with the speed of a runaway freight train, he set to work finishing the eleventh book in the Sidewinder Series: *Mad-Dog Pete Returns.*

He worked steadily for five hours, pausing only briefly to eat a sandwich Margie brought in. He thanked her for the tall and refreshing glass of lemonade that accompanied his lunch, but the moment she left the room he opened a drawer in the file cabinet and extracted a silver flask. He poured a generous belt of whiskey into the lemonade.

As the light bled from the day, Grant began the final chapter of the book; the shoot-out between the outlaw Mad-Dog Pete and Sheriff Dearborn. It would end with a bullet in the sheriff's chest, and Mad-Dog limping back to his horse with a gunshot wound to the leg. He would win the gunfight, but Grant didn't have the heart to let the outlaw ride away unscathed. He just couldn't kill off Dearborn without allowing him one small victory against the man that gunned him down in the middle of Main Street.

Grant didn't realize how hard it would be to write the sheriff's death. He was surprised to find his eyes moist and his hands hesitating to type the words. He pulled the flask from the file cabinet again.

It was nearly midnight before Grant imbibed enough whiskey to perform the dastardly deed of killing the man who had preserved law and order in Sidewinder South Dakota for the past seven years.

With a heavy heart, he slurred "I'll miss you, buddy," and turned off the computer.

As Grant emerged bleary-eyed from his office, the siren song of one last nightcap—just to drink a toast to the dearly departed sheriff—was too strong to deny. He wandered into the dining room, where a well-stocked bar sat in the corner like a welcoming friend, and poured a drink.

It was good scotch and it would be enjoyed from a Waterford glass. The sheriff deserved nothing less.

The following morning Grant awoke to a quiet house. His wife and daughter had left early to attend a craft fair and Grant had the morning to himself. He also had a miserable headache and decided the best cure would be a Bloody Mary. Light on the blood—heavy on the Mary.

He carried the drink to his office and sipped it while enjoying the view of the fairway. Once he was pleasantly numb, he fired up his email and sent Marta the completed manuscript of Mad-Dog Pete Returns to defragment his sentences and snip his dangling participles. He then composed a message to Emery Cleary:

From: SnakeMan@skynet.com
To: EmeryC@WesleyHouse.net
Subject: The Eagle Has Landed

Em,

Sorry for the delay in finishing the latest installment in the Sidewinder series. It is now in Marta's capable hands. Thanks for your patience. Today I am hard at work on book #12. This one won't be late, I promise.

Grant

Good to his word, Grant began the next book in the series by writing about Sheriff Dearborn's funeral. The whole town turned out to pay their respects and offer condolences to the widow Minnie, the kids, Rosie and Jess, and the Sheriff's mother, Grannie Annie. Even the Midnight Riders attended the service, standing a respectable distance apart from the grieving townsfolk. Deputy Starr arranged a posse to go find that vicious scoundrel Mad-Dog Pete, and see to it he was hanged.

Two weeks later, after Marta had worked her editorial magic, and the eleventh book in the Sidewinder series was put to bed, Grant received a most puzzling email from his publisher:

From: EmeryC@WesleyHouse.net
To: Snakeman@skynet.com
Subject: I Knew It

Hey Buddy,

I knew you couldn't go through with it. Sometimes I think you love that bow-legged sumbitch more than you do Margie. I'm not complaining; the ending was beautiful, even if Dearborn will live to fight another day after all. L'Amour has nothing on you, my friend.

Em

Grant looked at the screen completely puzzled. He read the note again, not understanding what his publisher was talking about. Dearborn would not live to fight another day. He was dead. He had given Emery advance warning of the sheriff's impending demise, so what on earth was he talking about?

Perplexed, Grant rubbed a hand across his mouth and scrolled back to the last email from Marta with the final edited copy of *Mad-Dog Pete Returns.*

He scrolled through the pages and read random sentences throughout the manuscript. Everything appeared to follow the story exactly as he wrote it. He stopped the random scan about three pages from the end and began reading more closely from the point where the shoot-out began:

Earlier in the day Mad-Dog had been seen bending an elbow with some boys at the Ace High Saloon. He'd apparently gotten full as a tick and was now spoiling for a fight.

The sheriff recognized the signs. That dull, flat look his eyes always got just before the shooting started. He tried to intervene before a fuss at the saloon began, but he was too late. Mort Feather, the hostler from upstate, accused Mad-Dog of cheating at the card table. He now lay dead with a .36 caliber slug in his head.

When Dearborn and Deputy Starr tried to diffuse the situation, it went from bad to worse. Mad-Dog started shooting at anything that moved. Most of the crowd made it out the swinging doors of the saloon or found cover under tables.

Earl the bartender took a slug in the arm, and a number of booze bottles disintegrated in a hail of gunfire sending shattered glass everywhere. One piece cut the pretty cheek of Miss Dolly. Deputy Starr, who had been sweet on her for years, rushed to her aid.

Now a crowd stood in front of the Ace High, every eye on Mad-Dog's fingers as they drummed restlessly above the well-oiled leather of his holster. The holster was second-hand and cracked with age. The man wore dingy dungarees, a stained shirt, and boots with the heels worn nearly off. Sheriff

Dearborn thought everything about Mad-Dog was second-hand. Except his shooting arm—that was first rate.

Grant couldn't help but smile when he read the last line. He'd loved it when he wrote it, and he loved it just as much now.

His eyes slipped further down the page to the gunfight between the sheriff and Mad-Dog Pete. He read a slight embellishment Marta had added to the description he'd written about the sound of screaming metal when another Colt slug was added to the bullet-riddled spittoon outside the swinging doors of the Ace High Saloon. He smiled at that, too.

Then all the color drained from Grant's face and he gasped. From that point on he was reading a book he had not written. The last two and a half pages of the manuscript sent to Marta for editing were gone. They were replaced by an ending Grant had never seen before. It was not only completely unrecognizable, it was an end to the book Grant had never even imagined.

He distinctly remembered writing a bullet fired into Dearborn's chest and ending his life. In Marta's version, the bullet intended for the sheriff's heart was lodged in his shoulder, and Mad-Dog was the one lying dead in the middle of Main Street as the sun set in the west. The book ended with Doc Wiffle disinfecting the wound in Dearborn's shoulder with 90 proof whiskey and setting to work to remove the slug. The sheriff was very much alive on the last page of *Mad-Dog Pete Returns*.

Grant's first reaction was fury. How could Marta take it upon herself to change his ending that way? She had never done such a thing before. Her edits always remained true to the story, and if there were content changes she really thought were necessary she always discussed them with Grant first. She would never make such a major change without his input. Never!

Yet, here it was. An ending completely different from the one Grant intended, and worse, it was far superior to anything he had ever written before. Emery was right—it was positively beautiful. He loved it more than the one he wrote himself.

It was high time Mad-Dog was taken out. He'd been getting liquored-up and shooting out the saloon for years now. It was tiresome. Grant wondered why he never thought to kill the bastard off himself.

His fury slowly dissolved. He didn't know Marta had that kind of creativity in her. She was always good for technical editing and embellishments to flesh out a description or a storyline, but he'd never seen her create anything from the ground up before. If she was such a talented writer, why was she wasting her gift editing other people's work instead of writing her own novels?

While the ending was great, and he would go with it—what choice did he have? The book was put to bed and headed for the press—he still intended to have a talk with her. She had grossly over-stepped, and Grant didn't want to see anything like this ever happen again.

When Marta answered the phone, Grant asked after her husband and kids. Once the pleasantries were out of the way he asked her pointedly, "Marta, didn't you think you should consult with me before altering the book so dramatically? I mean, the new ending completely screws up what I had planned for the next two books in the series. I will have to come up with a completely different storyline now."

There was silence on the line as Marta digested this. Finally she said, "Uh, Grant, I have no idea what you're talking about. I didn't change the ending. I loved it, in fact. I didn't rewrite a single word."

Grant felt a nasty ripple of fright creep up his spine. He knew he had been pretty drunk when he finished writing the book. Was it possible he changed the ending himself and didn't remember doing it? Was he really that far gone?

He mumbled something unintelligible to Marta about needing new reading glasses and hurried off the phone.

His hands were shaking as he opened up the documents file in his computer where he stored the un-edited copies of the Sidewinder books. He opened the completed manuscript he sent to Marta for editing. Grant stared in horrified wonder at the last page. It did not end in the sheriff's death. It ended exactly the same as the copy Marta returned. She had been telling the truth. Grant hadn't killed him after all.

He searched in vain for the pages he had written of the next book in the series. What had he done with them? That funeral was a real tear-jerker.

It was gone. There was nothing in his computer for book twelve. No funeral, no hunt for Mad-Dog. No start to the next book at all.

Grant was sure he must be losing his mind. Either that or he really had gone off the rails from the booze. He stumbled out of his office and did the only thing he could think of to steady his nerves. He took a drink.

Grant's wife didn't care much one way or the other about the fate of Sheriff Dearborn. She did, however, care a great deal about Grant's fate, and she didn't like where it appeared to be heading. She ignored the drinking as long as she could, but once he confided to her about not remembering changing the ending of the book,

Margie knew the situation was out of control. Something would have to be done.

On a rainy Saturday night, Grant stumbled from the country club. After several wrong turns through his neighbor's yards, and spending a futile ten minutes trying to open Mr. Murdoch's front door with his own house key, Grant finally, and quite miraculously, negotiated his way home. There were leaves caught in his hair, he was drenched head to toe, and his shoes were missing.

Grant weaved his unsteady way toward the den. He fell more or less in the direction of the couch and missed it entirely. Over-turning a potted plant, he passed out beside the coffee table and pulled the expensive Turkish area rug over his freezing body like a blanket.

His wife found him that way the following morning and shook him awake. She grimaced as Grant breathed a rank mist of day old scotch directly into her face.

"There's coffee in the kitchen," Margie said. "Why don't you go get cleaned up and bring a cup out to the patio. The kids and I will be waiting. We need to talk."

Penny, Grant's daughter from his first marriage, lived with them. She was in her first year at the local university. His son from the same union had been on his own for over two years and lived three-hundred miles away.

"Bobby's here?" Grant asked his wife, a puzzled frown creas-ing his brow.

After showering and brushing the rancid, unpleasant film from his teeth, Grant poured himself a cup of coffee. As he walked from the kitchen he glanced at the bar in the dining room. It stood completely empty. There was not a single bottle of liquor on the polished wood cabinet. The previous day the shelves were lined with over two dozen assorted spirits.

Margie's cryptic "we need to talk" comment coupled with the desolate bar was not a good sign. Grant felt a sinking feeling in his stomach. He walked warily out to the patio like a man approaching his own execution. He could see all the way to the ninth green from here and loved the view, but that wasn't what he was looking at now.

The spare folding chairs kept in the garage had been brought out and were arranged in a semi-circle on the patio. His wife and kids were there, and so was an attractive couple Grant did not recognize.

The woman held a brochure of some kind in her hand, and there was a briefcase leaning against the man's chair. They both wore professional looking suits. Grant wondered if Margie was finally at the end of her rope, and this pair was her divorce attorneys.

Of course, this wouldn't explain the presence of his children. He doubted his son would drive three hundred miles just to watch his father get served with divorce papers. He looked at the group suspiciously. Sighing, he arranged his face into what he hoped was an expression of polite interest, and walked out the door to join them.

His daughter looked as though she'd been crying. He could see a wadded up tissue clutched in her hand. Margie had a protective arm wrapped around the girl's shoulder. His son Bobby looked grim and wouldn't meet his eyes.

As the strangers rose from their chairs, the man reached out to shake Grant's hand. He introduced himself as Mr. Kirby, and his associate as Ms. Lang.

The polite expression Grant had tried so valiantly to maintain slipped from his face and he ignored the man's extended hand. Glaring at his wife, Grant barked, "What's this all about, Marge?"

He hated the wounded betrayal he heard in his voice, but was helpless to stop it. He felt like he was being ambushed.

Tears sprang to his wife's eyes when she heard his accusatory tone. "Grant, please sit down. There is something me and the kids need to say."

He started to back away from the group. They had ceased to look like his family, and now resembled a line of hungry vultures waiting to attack.

He nearly made it to the door, when Mr. Kirby placed one very meaty, strong hand on his arm and restrained him. Grant's coffee cup slipped from his grasp and landed on the ground between them, splashing coffee onto both men's shoes.

When Grant bent to retrieve the fallen cup, Kirby's grip tightened on his arm. The man's kind voice didn't match the vice-like grip he had on Grant's shoulder, as he said, "Please, Mr. Hudson, just leave that and sit down. Your family loves you and they want to help you."

"Help me what? I don't need any help!" Grant exclaimed in a voice so shrill he couldn't even convince himself it was true.

Kirby nudged him toward a chair. Grant was vaguely aware of the rippling of the man's bicep beneath his jacket. It looked like a boulder. Grant wearily dropped into the chair.

Kirby was roughly the size and strength of a gorilla. Grant knew he could neither outrun nor win a fight against him. He was going to have to sit through whatever hell his family had planned for him, or risk being manhandled by the goon with the nice gentlemanly voice again. He glared at his wife with bitter resentment.

Margie unfolded a piece of paper and began reading. "Grant, I love you, and I cannot watch you kill yourself this way. Your drinking has gotten out of control. This is an intervention…"

She went on to cite all the ways in which Grant was ruining their lives and their marriage by his alcohol abuse. When she got to the part about fearing for his sanity due to the book ending he did not remember writing, Grant realized she was probably right. He began to cry.

His daughter handed him a tissue and took his hand. Then she and his son also read carefully prepared, and blessedly brief, statements. When they were done, Mr. Kirby extracted what looked like a contract from his briefcase. There was a ballpoint pen clipped to the paper.

His associate handed Grant the brochure she had been holding and began explaining its significance.

The facility was called "The New Tomorrow Treatment Center." She and Mr. Kirby were there to escort him to rehab, where he would spend the next thirty days drying out.

While they didn't come right out and say that his commitment was involuntary, the sheer size of the man sent to accompany him left little doubt that his family intended to see him into that place, whether he wanted to go or not.

In the end he agreed, and fought the urge to call his wife a filthy name when she produced a suitcase already packed for his trip.

Like the new and improved ending for *Mad-Dog Pete Returns*, rehab might be a good idea, but it should have been his decision. He could not suppress the resentment rising in his chest like bile, as he was led away from his house and loaded into a van waiting at the curb.

PART TWO

Grant emerged from rehab the following month ten pounds lighter, clearer of mind and healthier of body. He was armed with an AA schedule and a new lease on life. His family rejoiced at his homecoming and he was anxious to return to work on the next book in the Sidewinder series.

During his absence Margie had converted the bar in the dining room into a plant stand. Grant, since returning home, had taken to tending to his wife's herb garden on the patio. It replaced his previous after-dinner activity of walking to the clubhouse and drinking.

Things with Margie were good, and he had spent the month in rehab wisely, by figuring out where to take the Sidewinder stories from here.

He really had no idea what direction to go in after the ending had changed on the last one so abruptly and without his knowledge. Grant remained deeply troubled by the whole event and it weighed on him. However, given the circumstances, he was forced to accept that in a drunken stupor he had indeed changed the book himself.

It still overwhelmed him that alcohol consumption could make him rewrite a book and not remember doing so. He could not even recall thinking up the alternate ending in the first place. Even now, he had absolutely no memory of dreaming up Mad-Dog Pete getting killed, or of deleting the several pages he began of the next book. He asked himself repeatedly why in the world he would ever have deleted such a beautifully written funeral. Not much caring for the uncomfortable light the answer shined on his mental health, he shoved it out of his mind.

Four months later, not plagued by anymore memory problems, Grant finished the thirteenth book in the series two weeks ahead of schedule and sent it off to Marta without incident.

He had shelved Sheriff Dearborn's demise for the time being. Having killed off one long-standing character in the last book, he didn't want to take Dearborn out now. Grant believed killing two established characters so close together might not sit well with his audience.

As it turned out, the thirteenth book in the Sidewinder series didn't sit well with the critics, let alone the readers. It was harshly reviewed. Critics threw around words like *ho-hum*, *predictable* and *leaden*. Grant was left wondering if minus the booze, he was actually a lousy writer.

He didn't mention this fear to his wife or his publisher. He faithfully stayed on the wagon and vowed to do better on book fourteen.

The notion of killing off Dearborn returned in the months ahead. Mad Dog, the sheriff's would-be assassin, was now dead, so Grant needed to come up with an entirely new storyline to end Dearborn's life. Since there was absolutely no one else in the entire town who would do such a dastardly thing, Grant was forced to introduce a new character into the Sidewinder community.

He created the McCafferty brothers; Derwin, a half-wit, and Donald, a hard drinking lady's man with a penchant for five-card stud.

Donald McCafferty promptly moved in on Johnny Starr's woman the moment his horse was tethered at the livery.

It was the idiot brother who would take out the sheriff, in what would be an unfortunate accident.

The first seventy-five pages of book fourteen, *Sins of the Brother,* were peppered with Derwin McCafferty's gaffes. Prone to accidents, they would include shooting off his own toe with his brother's Derringer, ripping Kitten the saloon girl's dress off by stepping on the hem, falling out a second story window, and knocking out one of Paddy the Cook's teeth with his elbow during a badly-timed run for the outhouse.

The readers wouldn't be terribly surprised when the unfortunate fool galloped his horse down Main Street and lost hold of the reins. The horse ran wild, throwing Derwin off, and ultimately trampling Dearborn to death.

Once more, Grant wrote the sheriff's funeral. It mirrored the one he remembered writing the first time, with all the townspeople turning out to comfort the family, and the Midnight Riders standing a respectful distance apart from the other mourners as Dearborn was laid to rest.

The book ended with Derwin McCafferty thrown in Sidewinder's tiny jail cell, and Deputy Starr trying to figure out what to do with him.

While Dearborn's death may have been an accident, the half-wit's brother was making time with Miss Dolly. The newly appointed sheriff wanted to make Donald McCafferty pay for stealing his woman. The son of a bitch had moved in on her right when Starr was preparing to propose. He had waited anxiously for six weeks for the ring to arrive from the Sears and Roebuck catalogue, intent on dropping to his knee and professing his undying love for Miss Dolly the moment he opened the package. Donald McCafferty had reduced those plans to rubble. The ring now sat in his bureau at home gathering dust, when where it should have been was on the finger of the lady he loved.

He would make McCafferty pay, and he could think of no better way than by punishing his brother.

Grant had visions of seeing Starr run the town with an iron fist in upcoming books. He pictured him doling out much harsher justice than his predecessor, and evolving from the mild-mannered sidekick he had been for the last decade. He would become a brute and a tyrant. Drunk on power, and determined to win back Miss Dolly, Starr would go to any lengths to show everyone who was in charge.

Who's ho-hum and predictable now? Grant thought as he wrote the final pages. *I'll show them!*

He did not tell Emery his plans for book fourteen. He also realized that writing Dearborn's death was much easier this time around. He needed no liquid courage to do the deed, and felt not the slightest pang of remorse or regret as he ended the book with Starr's fiery gaze resting on the half-wit's back, as he languished in the Sidewinder jail cell.

Grant and his wife returned from a walk. Margie went to the kitchen to fix them some lunch, while Grant went into his office to check email. Marta had sent the fully edited copy of *Sins of the Brother*. Her short note read, *Grant, another superb ending! Emery will be so pleased.*

Grant smiled proudly, and said, "Yeah, that's right. Superb!" He scrolled to the end of the book to bask in the glory of his superb finish, and began reading.

The last ten pages Grant distinctly remembered writing were gone. They were replaced by an extended tale of the love-triangle surrounding Miss Dolly. The final pages were of a drunken and heartsick Johnny Starr going after Donald McCafferty at the Ace High, and sending a poker table flying. It culminated in a wild bar-room brawl, that ended only after Sheriff Dearborn and Earl the bartender peeled the bloody and bruised men off the saw-dust covered floor and stopped them from pummeling each other.

The sheriff wasn't dead, no run-away horse trampled him on Main Street, and there was certainly no funeral.

Grant felt his heart seize up in his chest and then begin galloping faster than Derwin's out of control horse in the version he remembered writing of *Sins of the Brother*.

He jumped from his desk chair and backed away from the computer like it was on fire. He was not aware he was screaming until Margie's footfalls thundered down the hallway and she burst into his office, still holding a spatula in one hand.

"Grant, what is it? What's wrong?" Taking in his pale face, and the hand clutching his chest, she rushed to his side. "Oh, God! Is it a heart attack? I'll call 911!"

Grant pointed at the computer with one accusatory finger, and shouted, "I did not write that!" He was trembling all over.

Margie followed his bulging eyes and outstretched finger. "You didn't write what?"

"Th...that!" he stammered, waving a hand wildly at the screen. "It's not my story, Margie! It's not what I sent to Marta. What the hell is going on here?"

Margie put a hand to her mouth and whispered, "Oh, Grant. Not this again. When did you fall off the wagon?"

When he turned his eyes on his wife, they were blazing with fury. "I didn't! How can you even ask me that? I haven't had a drink since the day you carted me off to that place last year."

Grant pulled the one year chip from Alcoholics Anonymous out of his pocket and threw it at his wife. He had earned it only the week before, and was extremely proud of it.

Margie watched in shock as Grant fled from the room. She heard the front door slam. Picking up the chip he had hurled at her, she collapsed weeping to his desk chair.

If ever Grant needed a drink, it was after reading the manuscript Marta returned for *Sins of the Brother*. Following the horrible fight with Margie, he ran to the nearest AA meeting.

Once it was over, and Grant felt more in control of himself, he needed to find somewhere to go and think. He wasn't ready to return home. He was startled to realize that he couldn't think of a single place to go for some quiet time besides a bar.

For the first time in over a year, he went to the Gatesville country club. He forced himself to walk inside, even though it felt like returning to the scene of a crime. The bartender greeted him like an old friend and masked his surprise well when Grant ordered ginger ale.

Okay, Grant thought, *here are my options. One: I have really and truly lost my mind. Two: I started drinking again at eleven o'clock this morning and don't remember doing it. Which would take us back to option one; I'm crazy.*

Grant knew there had been no alcohol in his system for over a year. Not so much as a single bottle of beer had passed his lips since he was released from the treatment center. He was not having any memory problems—nor was he hallucinating or crazy.

It was with an overwhelming sense of relief that Grant realized the last time this happened wasn't his doing either. He accepted what had happened then because alcohol was not only his constant companion during that time, it was also a convenient way to explain an ending to one of his books that he never thought up, let alone wrote. It was far more palatable than the alternative: he'd lost his mind.

He knew there probably wasn't enough alcohol in the western hemisphere to cause him to rewrite the ending of *Mad-Dog Pete Returns*. It was neither insanity nor alcoholism which changed the fate of Sheriff Dearborn. Somebody else rewrote the ending to both books, it was that simple.

This could mean that Marta was the one who was crazy, but Grant didn't think so. So who did it?

He couldn't come up with any reason why someone would hack his computer and rewrite the ending to his books, unless there was some crazy, computer savvy fan out there who just couldn't bear to see Dearborn die. Oddly, as far-fetched as that scenario seemed, it made the most sense. And really, how much of a stretch was it? Grant's computer was probably a lot easier to hijack than Sony Pictures, and some cyber-attacker managed to break into the movie behemoth's system with no problem at all.

He absolutely could not tell Emery about this. Judging by his wife's reaction, he was pretty sure the consensus would be the same. The last thing he needed was Kirby the bruiser showing up with his girlfriend again to cart him back to rehab. For all he knew Margie might have called them the minute he ran out the front door after their quarrel. He had no choice but to let the book go to print the way it was, and try to get to the bottom of this mystery himself.

First, he needed to return home and do some damage control with his wife.

Margie rushed to the front door as soon as she heard Grant's key in the lock. When he opened the door she flung her arms around him.

"I was so worried," she sobbed.

"I haven't been drinking, if that's what you were worried about," Grant replied.

"I'm so sorry, Grant. I never should have assumed that. It was just like déjà vu when you were yelling about the book, and I just thought…"

"It's alright, honey. Come sit down. I need to talk to you."

"Is this the part where you ask me for a divorce?"

"No. This is the part where I ask you to keep an open mind and trust me."

He laid out his theory about the cyber-attack, and was relieved when his wife embraced the idea. He supposed she was grateful for any notion that didn't circle back to the conclusion that he was drinking again.

It was little consolation how well the critics received *Sins of the Brother*. One reviewer was quoted as saying, "Just like Stella, Grant got his groove back."

Grant thought that was the stupidest thing he ever heard, but was secretly very relieved no words like ho-hum or leaden were in any of the latest reviews. The critics, as well as the readers, apparently loved the new characters Grant introduced, and they particularly liked the love-triangle between the deputy, Donald McCafferty and Miss Dolly. Grant started thinking maybe his cyber-attacker was smarter than he was. It was probably a good idea to allow the readers the chance to get to know the McCafferty brothers before turning one of them into the instrument of Sheriff Dearborn's demise.

Grant called a friend with the police department and explained that he was worried his computer had been hacked. He was given the name of a forensic computer specialist to call.

The specialist spent five days combing through Grant's hard drive and could find no evidence anything had been breached or tampered with.

While the news was frustrating, Grant still believed his system had been compromised. The hacker was obviously extremely sophisticated and left no cyber-fingerprint behind.

He bought a new computer and changed internet providers. He could think of nothing else to do to block future attacks, short of going back to typing his manuscripts on his old Olivetti. Book fifteen needed to be written, and Grant was more determined than ever to see Sheriff Dearborn dead.

His plans had not changed. Fortunately the altered ending of *Sins of the Brother* did not require him to deviate from the story going forward. The next book would pick up right where the last one left off.

Grant would add a few more mishaps for Derwin McCafferty to remind the readers of what an accident prone fool he was, and then mow Dearborn down with the imbecile's horse on Main Street exactly the way he meant for it to go in the last book. That damn funeral was going to take place one way or another and there wouldn't be a dry eye in the house.

Grant wrote the Sheriff's death with grim determination. He felt a strange sense of glee as he described Dearborn's mangled body lying in the middle of Main Street.

When book fifteen, *A Starr Rises in the West,* was finished, Grant saved it to a flash drive and put it in his pocket. He was ten days ahead of schedule, but did not send the book to Marta for editing just yet. He wanted to wait and see if his cyber-stalker planned on paying his new computer a visit first.

He woke the morning after completing the book and went into his office. His heart gave an uncomfortable lurch when he saw the chair had been pushed away from his desk and the computer left on. Grant distinctly remembered shutting it down and tucking the chair against the desk before retiring the night before. On the carpet were muddy footprints leading from the patio door to the desk. There was a matched set in reverse.

The police were called in. They were instantly suspicious of Grant. With no sign of forced entry, and the alarm failing to sound when the intruder gained entry into the house, it was difficult to accept that anyone had broken in at all. Were it not for the muddy footprints, the officers would have left without even taking a report. Margie convinced them to dust for fingerprints and take photos of the footprints.

When Grant pulled up the manuscript for *A Starr Rises in the West*, everything after chapter three was gone. Not rewritten—completely erased. The rest of the book from that point on had dealt with the Sheriff's death, the funeral, and Johnny Starr. The book mostly centered on the scorned lover's rise to power, and his ugly transformation from mild-mannered deputy to the worst sheriff Sidewinder had ever seen in the months following Dearborn's death.

Grant planned to overnight the flash drive to Marta for editing soon, but first he was determined to find out who was playing this dangerous game with his books.

The fingerprints taken by the police matched no one besides Grant and his family. Everyone secretly wondered if Grant wasn't drinking again, and suffering the effects with the granddaddy of all hallucinations. No one said this to his face. Especially not Margie, who tried very hard to believe her husband was not responsible for what was happening, despite incriminating evidence to the contrary.

Grant had a plan. He checked the flash drive to make sure it contained the entire manuscript. Next he sat down at the computer and began to retype the killing of Sheriff Dearborn. He didn't think he would need to write any more than that. He saved the pages and turned off the computer.

That night, after Margie fell asleep, Grant returned to his office and hid behind the desk. At some point he dozed off. He was awakened by the squeak of the wheels on his desk chair.

His heart leapt into his throat. He heard the computer whir to life in the darkness. Next fingers were tapping at the keyboard. He sat motionless, terrified of being discovered in his hiding place, mere inches from where the intruder worked.

A few minutes later the chair wheels squeaked again and footsteps retreated toward the patio door. Grant peeked under the desk, but could see nothing in the gloom. He did not hear the patio door open and had no idea where the prowler had gone. He was terrified the person might have gone into the main part of the house.

On shaking legs Grant rose from his hiding place. He brandished a bowling trophy from a shelf before giving chase. He knew he should call 911, but fear for the safety of his daughter and wife prevented him from taking the time to make the call.

He tiptoed through the quiet house and found no one. His wife and Penny slept soundly in their beds. After checking every room, Grant returned to his office and turned on the light.

He stared in wonder at two sets of footprints, identical to the ones just cleaned up the previous day. One set leading from the patio to the desk, the other going the opposite direction.

With a shaking hand Grant reached for the computer mouse and opened *A Starr Rises in the West*. As he suspected, the pages he rewrote were gone.

The intruder could not have accessed the house without tripping the alarm. They had changed the code and no one besides Grant and his family had the new number. It seemed as though who ever broke in had simply disappeared like smoke. The footprints left behind were baffling. Grant would have heard the intruder exit through the patio door while he hid behind the desk. He heard the chair pushed from the desk when the trespasser finished deleting the pages of the book he came to get rid of. Then he just vanished.

The footprints may have told a different story, but Grant had been right there. He knew the person never walked out the patio door. Clearly he hadn't gone into the house either. So where was he?

The word "supernatural" floated through Grant's mind like a message trailing behind a blimp.

As a writer of fiction about the Old West, not weird ghost stories taking place in haunted manors, the word looked foreign floating across his brain like that. He never really gave much thought to poltergeists, ghosts or any of their distant cousins like zombies and werewolves. The word *supernatural* was unwelcome, yet strangely alluring.

He decided not to call the police to report another break-in. On further introspection he decided not to tell his wife about what happened either. Grant wasn't sure a tale like this would be believable to anyone, even if his past did not include a stint in rehab.

While fiction writers, by sheer virtue of their craft, were expected to hear the occasional voice in their heads, Grant figured the line was probably drawn at seeing computer-hacking ghosts who left muddy footprints behind. That was the type of thing that bought a fellow a ticket straight into the funny-farm—or in his case, back to rehab by way of a big guy named Kirby and his girlfriend Ms. Lang.

PART THREE

Grant's wife and daughter were attending some yoga workshop in the city. They would be gone over night. Grant waited until he was alone in the house before rewriting the sheriff's death a third time and saving the pages to his hard drive.

Tonight he planned on confronting his stalker face to face. Grant had no doubt the one who refused to let Sheriff Dearborn die would show up again. He hadn't disappointed yet.

Grant was scared half to death, and if ever there was a good time to fall off the wagon and drink a little liquid courage, now was it. But he would stay strong and he would deal with this thing once and for all, whether it be man or ghost.

Grant watched the sunset from his patio. The longing for a drink was stronger than Mr. Kirby's ape-like hands, as he watched the sun steal behind the horizon.

He went inside and drank a cup of completely unsatisfying tea, as he waited for night to take hold, and the dreaded confrontation he knew lie ahead.

Midnight turned into one AM with no sign of Dearborn's savior. Finally Grant dozed.

He was awakened by the increasing breeze outside. The wind blew something hard and rattling against the house. Rising from his desk chair, Grant's eyes began adjusting to the dark. He thought he must be dreaming when he looked outside. Beyond the patio, the golf course had disappeared. His jaw sagged open when he realized what he was seeing. It was Main Street in Sidewinder. The dusty road, exactly as he had been writing it for nearly the last decade, was now right outside the back of his house. Across the street he could see the swinging doors to the saloon, and the oil lamps from inside cast a dim yellow glow on the spittoon out front.

As Grant watched in awe, a tumbleweed skated across his patio, catching on one of the plants in Margie's herb garden.

Grant hoped like hell he was dreaming, as he watched the doors of the Ace High swing open and Sheriff Dearborn walk out into the street. With single minded purpose, the lawman strode across Main Street and stepped onto Grant Hudson's patio.

Grant rose from the desk chair and began backing across the room. His heart was hammering in his chest and he broke out in a clammy sweat.

He tried to remember if somewhere during the long night he had given in to the miserable craving and found a bottle of booze somewhere. Glancing at the half empty teacup on his desk, he knew he hadn't. Booze wasn't causing this hallucination. It was either real, or he had completely lost his mind.

Grant decided if he was crazy, he needed to know that. However, if this was real, he needed to flee from the advancing lawman before he reached the back door.

Making up his mind, Grant stopped where he stood and waited for Sheriff Dearborn to come inside.

The two men stood staring at each other across the room. It was Dearborn who broke the silence first. "You and me need to have us a talk, Ol' Hoss."

Shit. He sounded exactly the way Grant had always heard his voice inside his own head. He looked exactly the way Grant described him in the books. Salt and pepper hair, gray sideburns, bow-legs wrapped in neatly pressed denims. The badge pinned at his breast sparkled, even in the bleak shadowy light of midnight. The sheriff always kept it polished to a bright shine. He was very finicky about his appearance. Grant had made him that way.

Grant tried to speak, "Wh…" nothing but a croak escaped his lips. His mouth had gone dry. He cleared his throat and tried again. "Why, um, why don't you have a seat." He waved absently toward a chair.

Dearborn shook his head. "I don't think so. I think we need to head on over to the Ace High and have a whiskey. Talk this over like men."

The whiskey sounded great to Grant. He wondered if having one in a fictitious town counted as falling off the wagon. What sounded even better was actually getting to walk into the saloon he created. He was dying to see Miss Dolly and Kitten up close. Watch Earl, as he slid a glass of amber whiskey across the bar.

He reminded himself he might still be crazy after all. "I can't do that, Wayne. I don't drink anymore."

"Hmm. Is that right? I never met a fella wouldn't bend an elbow and work things out like a gentleman before, but we'll do it your way… for now."

The sheriff dropped into a chair and waved for Grant to sit down.

Grant plopped into his office chair. "So, what brings you here?"

"Oh, come on, Ol' Hoss. I think you know the answer to that. You been tryin' to kill me for months. I can't believe you was gonna let that no good, second-hand sumbitch, Mad-Dog, take me out in the middle of God-dern Main Street. Talk about bitin' the hand that feeds yah."

Grant stared at Dearborn and rubbed his eyes. He pinched his arm, to see if he would wake up from this nightmare.

"Well, ain't you gonna say somethin'? 'Cause the way I see things one of us is gonna die. And I got news, Ol' Hoss. It ain't gonna be me." Dearborn said, crossing his arms stubbornly over his chest.

"Um… Well, you see, I am having a little trouble with this whole thing," Grant said. "Has it really been you who changed the books? How can you do that? You… you aren't even real. I created you."

"Yeah, and now you is tryin' to kill me. What kind of a papa kills his own youngins'? It ain't natural."

"I'm not your papa."

"Well, you ain't gonna be my assassin neither. So what's it gonna be? You or me? You already know I can write them books nearly better than you can. Who'd know the difference once you was gone?"

"This can't be happening."

"Come on, buddy. Let's go on over to the Ace High and have a drink. You look pale as a polecat at the business end of a rifle. I think you could use one." Dearborn rose from the chair and walked to the patio door.

Grant followed him outside. He looked at the tumbleweed caught in the herb garden and watched it flash into a vague outline, like the negative of a photograph. A moment later it solidified once more. The air was uncomfortably thick and charged with static, the same way it felt just before an electrical storm. He suddenly understood that if he left the safety of his patio and stepped onto Main Street with the sheriff, he would never return to Gatesville. He'd be trapped in Sidewinder for good.

"No," Grant said, "I'm not going there. I don't belong there. You can't make me go."

The sheriff shocked him by pulling his five-shot Paterson revolver from the holster at his hip and pointing it at him. "Don't be so sure, Ol' Hoss."

Grant sagged against the patio door. A sheriff born of his imagination was pointing a gun he had painstakingly created— after doing extensive research about firearms used by lawmen in the Old West—right at him.

He was being threatened by a character in a book. This couldn't be happening. Grant felt like some kind of real-life Dr. Frankenstein; his creation had just come to life and turned on him. If Dearborn shot him would there be actual bullets? Would he really die? That was a chance he wasn't willing to take.

"Okay, just calm down. Let's go back inside and work this out. Put the gun away, okay, Wayne?"

The sheriff hesitated for a moment, thinking. Finally he lowered the revolver and put it back in the holster. "Fine, but only 'cause I can't stay much longer. Minnie and the kids will be wonderin' where the hell I am. Min already thinks I'm two-timin' her, cause I have to keep runnin' out at night to prevent you from killin' me. This has gotta stop."

Grant opened his mouth to speak, but the sheriff wasn't done yet. "And what the hell are you doin' to Johnny? He's a good boy. Why you tryin' to turn him into a bully? Ain't it bad enough what you done to his love-life?"

Grant closed his eyes. He decided if he got out of this alive, he was going to find a bottle of booze somewhere. He had earned a drink tonight for sure.

He reached behind him and opened the door. Ushering Dearborn inside, he sat down hard at his desk.

"What is it you want me to do exactly, Wayne."

"Ain't that obvious? Quit tryin' to kill me. Write somethin' else. Do it, or I am gonna take you out. And maybe your perty little wife, too. I'm serious, Hoss. This bullshit stops now."

Grant nodded. "Alright, Wayne. I'll change the story."

Once the sheriff threatened Margie, Grant's blood ran cold. He didn't know how the hell a character in a book could come to life, and frankly he didn't want to know, but this one had pointed a gun at him. He was not going to see his family put at risk. Now he really wished he were crazy. He would rather be insane than see Margie suffer because he killed off a character in a book.

"So, we understand each other? You'll quit this foolishness now?" Dearborn asked.

"Absolutely. I will write a new story tomorrow for the next book. You will be very much alive. Okay? Are we good?"

The sheriff nodded. "I'm glad you come to see reason." He rose to leave. As he was walking out the back door he paused. "One more thing."

"What's that?" Grant asked nervously.

"If anyone ought to have an accident, it's that low-down Donald McCafferty. Give Johnny back Miss Dolly. The boy is miserable. Breaks my heart to see him like that."

Dearborn did not wait for Grant to respond. He closed the door behind him. Grant watched him vanish in thin air as he stepped off the patio and onto Main Street. The town of Sidewinder disappeared with him. When Grant glanced at Margie's herb garden the tumbleweed was gone.

Grant sat at his desk for a long time after Dearborn left. "If I were crazy, I think I'd know it," he said to the empty office. "I don't know how it happened, but Sheriff Dearborn came to life."

Upon making that great realization, he muttered, "Damn lucky I didn't write about vampires. I'd probably be lying here dead with my blood drained out."

The question was, how could he get rid of him? He realized Dearborn knew nothing about the flash drive he still had. The original story in which the sheriff was killed was safely hidden inside a box of cereal in his pantry right now. How could he get that over to Marta without Sheriff Dearborn knowing? If the book went to print, Grant was confident the sheriff could do nothing about it. He would have to die.

Weary from exhaustion, and strangely, not craving a drink any longer, Grant rose from his desk. He paused for a moment and looked out into the gloom, fully expecting to see Main Street and the gas lamps aglow in the Ace High Saloon. When it was just the golf course outside, he extinguished the light and went to bed. A plan was starting to come together in his mind. He thought he just might know how to get rid of the character in his book that refused to die after all.

The following day, Grant welcomed Margie and his daughter home. They ate a late brunch and then he retired to his office to write.

He wrote the first forty pages of a completely changed version of book fifteen. If Dearborn looked into his computer tonight, and Grant knew he would, he would be satisfied with what he read. The sheriff's heart was beating, there were no tragic accidents and no one came gunning for him.

On Monday morning Grant needed to make an awkward and uncomfortable phone call to Emery. He didn't want to make the call, but for his plan to work there was no choice.

He drove into town and searched for a payphone. He had to drive for over forty-five minutes to locate one. With everyone owning cellphones, there weren't many left anymore.

While Grant was pretty sure Dearborn couldn't tap his cellphone, he wasn't going to take any chances. The sheriff shouldn't have been capable of rewriting his books—or showing up at his house with the entire town of Sidewinder behind him either for that matter.

After several frustrating minutes spent fumbling with entering his credit card information, the call was finally connected.

"Hey, Em. It's Grant. I have um… well, a kind of odd request, and I am going to need you to humor me."

There was silence on the line as Emery Cleary absorbed this declaration. "Is there a problem with the book, Grant? Do you need an extension?" *Or rehab again?* the publisher thought, but did not say.

"Not a problem, really. I'm just… well, a little superstitious. I don't want any email communication sent to my computer about the book from you or Marta. I am going to send you a flash drive with the book on it, and I want you to hand it to Marta in person. When she's done editing, I want her to reload it to that same flash drive and hand it back to you. It can't be saved on anyone's computer."

Emery Cleary had worked with a great many successful authors. He knew that they were all a little eccentric. He had stopped questioning them about their odd proclivities long ago. Most were half crazy anyway, so why bother. This one was not only half crazy, he was also an alcoholic. This request, while strange and out of the ordinary, really wasn't a big deal.

"Sure, Grant. No problem."

Grant breathed a huge sigh of relief. "Thanks, Em, I really appreciate this. There is one more thing."

"What's that?"

"I don't want to see the edited book until it's released. I don't even want to talk about it. If you need to get in touch with me about anything pertaining to book fifteen, just leave me a message on my cellphone to call you. Don't use your name. Just leave a two-word message, 'call me,' okay? Don't say anything more than that, alright?"

Emery distinctly remembered Joshua Jones, a science fiction author he worked with about ten years ago. Joshua got the strange notion in his head that aliens were after him and had tapped his phones. The poor guy grew so paranoid he started wearing tinfoil hats, and refused to watch the television because he thought extraterrestrials could watch him back through the screen. He eventually committed suicide.

Emery sincerely hoped Grant wouldn't meet the same sad ending. He was a good writer and a nice man. Emery genuinely liked him.

"Grant, I have to ask. Do you need some help? Someone to talk to, maybe? Are you still sober?"

"I'm not falling apart, and I'm not drinking, I swear. If I could explain what was going on, I would. After this book, things should be back to normal. At least I hope so. If they aren't, the Sidewinder series will be over anyway, so it won't matter."

Now Emery was alarmed. "What do you mean over? You still have a contract."

Grant gave a rueful laugh. "Don't worry, Em. I wouldn't breach my contract. I love writing the books. It would be over because I will be dead. You see, there is a lot riding on this book, so please just remember what I asked. Don't let Marta save the edited book to her hard drive. Only to the flash I am sending over, and it needs to be taken out of the computer and hidden in a safe place every night when she is done working on the manuscript. It can't stay plugged into the port in her computer ever. Tell her to finish it as fast as possible. And absolutely no phone calls, okay?"

"Sure, Grant. I got it. If you need… well you know… if you need anything… anything at all, give me a call alright? I'm worried about you."

"Don't be, I think everything will be okay, Em. You just need to do what I ask, even if you think it sounds crazy."

"Okay, Grant. I will, you have my word. Is there anything else?"

"Yes. Tell Marta I am going to be sending her over another version of book fifteen via email. It won't be the one that is going to press, but I need her to do just a few minor edits here and there and send it back to me a week later. That way, things will look normal. The real book fifteen will be the one on the flash drive. The copy she gets in her email is a… well, it's a decoy."

Emery, sounding totally baffled, asked, "Why do you need a decoy book?"

"Don't ask, Em. Please just do this for me. I promise after this book everything will go back to the way it was."

Grant hoped that was true.

Day after day, Grant wrote the new story on his computer. There were no more nocturnal visits from Sheriff Dearborn, and the story remained as he wrote it.

In the meantime, he put the flash drive with the story he intended to go to press into an envelope and drove to the post office. He sent it overnight express to Emery. He made sure that Emery personally had to sign for the delivery.

He used a computer at the library to check the tracking number of the package the next day to see that it was delivered.

Once finished with the decoy copy of book fifteen, Grant sent it to Marta via email with a short note. He hoped like hell she wouldn't write him back, asking what the hell it was. He was praying Emery kept his word and had alerted her to expect this one.

For seven days Grant held his breath. On the eighth day he received back the edited copy of the decoy from Marta with a standard note praising his work. Grant almost sobbed with relief when he read it.

Emery had done what he asked, and everything was going according to plan. Now all he could do was wait.

The book would be released in sixty-two days. He would find out in just over two months whether or not his plan had worked. He spent each and every day of those months looking out the window and expecting to see Sheriff Dearborn striding across Main Street, but it never happened.

A Starr Rises in the West was met with rave reviews. Margie noticed Grant was unusually subdued when he read the critics accolades. "Why aren't you thrilled?" she asked him.

"I am, hon. Just waiting to see what tomorrow brings."

Margie looked puzzled. "What could tomorrow bring that's any different? It's obvious they love it."

"It's not the critics I'm worried about."

Thinking she understood, his wife replied, "Oh, Grant, your readers will love it, too. Don't worry."

That night, Grant slept little. He spent most of the night tossing and turning, listening for any suspicious noise. He knew the possibility existed that if a living character from a book could visit him in the wee hours of the night, then that character's ghost might be able to visit after he was dead as well. He would know by morning if his plan had worked, and he had outsmarted Sheriff Dearborn.

At nine o'clock the following day he steeled himself to face the computer.

Nothing was amiss. The sheriff had not come gunning for him in the night. Dearborn was really gone.

It took a month for Grant to accept that the nightmare was truly over, and start sleeping through the night again. He was always surprisingly relieved when he looked out his office window and saw nothing but the ninth green beyond.

Three months passed, and Grant was getting ready to set to work on book sixteen.

The morning he went to his office to begin writing, he saw a note taped to the front of his computer monitor. It was handwritten, and said:

> Hey Ol' Hoss,
>
> Don't go gettin' no funny ideas 'bout killin' me, you hear? I won't be fooled as easy as Dearborn was, and I plan on bein' sheriff 'round these parts for a long time. Remember now, I'm watchin' you.
>
> Signed,
> Sheriff John Starr

A CASE OF MISTAKEN IDENTITY

RICHARD FREEMAN ONLY caught the last thirty seconds or so of the lead story on the evening news. The number sixteen bus was late or he would have seen the whole thing, complete with the crew and field reporter dispatched to the scene of the crime for live coverage. As it turned out, he saw enough.

Richard stood slack-jawed, staring in shock at the police artist's rendering of the suspect splayed across his television, before it, and the reporter with the too-perfect teeth, were replaced by a dancing box of laundry detergent skipping across the screen.

He had missed the details of the crime, catching only enough of the story to learn one thing: He knew the identity of the suspect in that drawing. It was his boss, Matt Gibson.

Richard unrolled the newspaper and read the headline on the first page. It was chilling:

OCEANSIDE STRANGLER VICTIM ESCAPES

He'd heard about the rash of murders taking place up and down the coastline. There was a serial killer on the loose. The media had dubbed him "The Oceanside Strangler." His victims: four pretty young women, found strangled and sexually assaulted. Their bodies discarded like trash on the beach.

The police had few leads and were disclosing scant information to the public. It was scary.

Scarier still, was who the likeness of the suspect resembled, right down to the mole underneath his right eye and the thin oddly shaped scar that kissed his upper lip.

The fifth victim had barely managed to escape and flag down a car as she fled up Pacific Coast Highway, half naked and frightened out of her mind. The assailant was nowhere in sight when someone stopped to render aid to the hysterical girl.

She managed to give authorities a detailed description of her attacker, which resulted in the sketch now blanketing the media.

Richard picked up the phone to call 911 and then paused. Could one make a reasonable assumption of guilt based only on an artist's rendering? What if that wasn't Matt? Did he really want to be the one responsible for accusing the wrong man of such dreadful crimes?

Richard set the phone down. Surely someone else who knew Matt must have seen the news coverage. He would let that presumed *someone else* report it. Matt had always been good to him. He was a great boss and a very nice man. Richard decided not to make the call.

The following day at the advertising firm where Richard worked, he tried to overhear every snippet of conversation to see if anyone else was talking about the odd similarities between that sketch of the Oceanside Strangler and Matt Gibson.

By noon, when nothing was gleaned from the surreptitious eavesdropping, Richard asked a fellow employee if he had seen the news story. The man's puzzled expression was answer enough.

He asked a secretary, but she only shook her head and shuddered at the subject matter.

That night the news declared leads were "pouring in" and a special hotline had been set up for people with any information to call. He was urged to phone the number at the bottom of the screen if he had anything worthwhile to share about the Oceanside Strangler's identity or whereabouts. There was now a ten-thousand dollar reward being offered for information leading to an arrest.

Still, Richard did not call. If leads were "pouring in," there was no doubt someone must have coughed up the name Matt Gibson by now. The resemblance was positively uncanny.

Matt was absent from work the following day. His secretary said he had called in sick. As Richard could not recall Matt taking more than two sick days in the past six years, he figured this must be it. Matt had been arrested. Richard would not have to make that call after all. Someone else had turned him in.

Richard remembered a night six months previously when he and Matt were having celebratory cocktails for landing a large account. Emboldened by the alcohol, Richard asked his boss about the scar on his lip. He had always wondered what caused the odd question mark shaped scar, but never thought it appropriate to ask.

Matt had laughed and rubbed it lightly with his thumb. "Oh, this. Well, when I was a kid I had a skateboard, and one day I decided it would be cool to ride that puppy down a steep flight of concrete steps. Needless to say, it was a bad idea. I took about twenty stitches and lost both front teeth." He tapped the veneers with a finger.

"Wow," Richard replied, not knowing what else to say.

His boss went on. "Right after it healed and we saw how bad the scar was, my folks thought I should have plastic surgery. But my friends thought it was cool—you know, like a badge of honor. And a few years after that I discovered the thing was a real chick-magnet. I sure didn't want to get rid of it then," he laughed. "Who knows, Laura might not have married me without the question mark on my lip."

Richard took a moment to take a mental inventory of his own physical anomalies. He could think of nothing on his entire person one would classify as a chick-magnet. Richard had always been an extraordinarily plain boy, and he grew into an equally uninspiring man. By thirty-five his hair was thinning, and his complexion, always easy to burn, no matter how high the SPF count on the sun-block he used, was pale to the point of looking sickly. Unlike his robust boss, who probably didn't need the chick-magnet scar any-way. Matt was tanned year round, had an unruly mop of brown curls that even Richard might have been tempted to run his fingers through, and a strong, well-toned physique. He drove a Porsche. Richard wondered if Matt knew he would have been a chick-mag-net even without the oddly shaped scar. Probably not—he was too humble to see it.

Richard was a little envious of Matt's easy good looks, his win-ning smile, (the veneers were probably an improvement over his real teeth,) his expensive sports car, and his beautiful family. Matt had it all, while a guy like him could never aspire to be anything more than a guy like Matt's wingman.

Richard struggled with women from an early age. In high school he lacked the courage to ask any girl to accompany him to the senior prom, so he went solo. Adulthood brought no improve-ment to the situation.

Earlier this year, in desperation, he joined an online dating site and met a woman named Denise.

Denise, with her organic diet and endless herbal remedies. Denise, with her turtleneck sweaters and ankle length skirts. Her lady-parts were guarded more fervently than the Hope Diamond. Denise claimed to be saving herself for "the right man." Richard had few illusions he would ever be Mr. Right, but still he hung in there.

The relationship lasted for three months before Denise abruptly broke up with him in an email. The few short sentences offered no explanation for her sudden departure from his life.

What ensued was a horribly embarrassing month. Richard phoned Denise hundreds of times and left countless messages on her voicemail. She returned his call only once, asking him to stop harassing her. When he didn't, she eventually changed her phone number. Richard continued to call and listen to the mechanical voice inform him that the number he had dialed was no longer in service.

Not long after their break-up the strange murders on the beach began. Richard found it rather disturbing that all the victims looked like Denise. Same hair color, same body type. *She better watch out,* Richard remembered thinking just after the third victim was found. He felt a little guilty for fantasizing about Denise being one of the unfortunate victims of the Oceanside Strangler.

It turned out that Matt was not absent from work because he was arrested. His six-year old daughter, Cara, had the flu. He stayed home because his wife had caught the same bug. "I was taking care of both my girls," he told Richard the next day.

Two weeks passed with Matt still skating under the police's radar, and without another murder. Richard prayed they were over for good. Alas, that was not to be. Another body was found on the beach. And then another.

The police were frantic for leads. Still Richard did not call. He could not turn Matt over the authorities without proof that he was indeed the Oceanside Strangler. He decided to find out once and for all by following his boss.

He feared this plan was possibly as foolish as Matt riding his skateboard down the concrete steps had been, but he didn't know what else to do.

Richard began his surveillance on a Thursday. He stayed parked across the street from Matt's house, slumped down in the car until after two AM. This continued until sleep-deprivation and back pain began to take too great a toll five nights later.

The surveillance proved futile. Matt never left his house after returning home from work on any of the nights Richard watched him. The only exception was one evening when he took his wife to dinner. Richard followed them to the restaurant. They returned just after eight-thirty, and Matt remained home for the rest of the night. No murders occurred the entire week Richard spied on his boss.

Just two nights after Richard gave up his surveillance another victim was found on the beach. Richard felt horrible. He knew it was time to report Matt. His conscience would not let him remain silent any longer. He decided against calling the tip-line. He assumed, quite correctly, that the police were sifting through hundreds of messages from that line. He couldn't wait. He knew he should have gone to them weeks ago.

The following evening when Richard got off work, he went to the police department and asked if he could speak to someone about the Oceanside Strangler. He told the duty officer he knew who the killer was.

The officer quickly led Richard to a small airless room with sparse furnishings. Moments later a burly detective appeared and introduced himself as Detective Pete Russell with the homicide division. He gave Richard a paper cup filled with water and set up a small portable tape recorder on the desk between them.

"You don't mind if I tape our conversation, Mr. Freeman, do you?" he asked.

Richard shook his head and the detective pressed the button to start the tape recording.

"Now, Mr. Freeman, what information do you have about the murder cases we are investigating?"

Richard was silent for so long that Russell began to reach out to stop the tape recorder. Richard finally blurted, "I think the Oceanside Strangler is my boss."

The detective raised his eyebrows and replied, "I see. Do you have any evidence to support this allegation?"

Richard pulled his cell phone from his pocket. He turned the phone toward the detective and showed him Matt's company photo. He had downloaded the image from the firm's website before coming to the police department. He pointed to the mole beneath his right eye and the unusual scar at his upper lip. "You see? Even the curly hair is the same." Richard's voice cracked and he cleared his throat.

The detective visibly paled as he looked at the picture on Richard's phone. He tapped the question mark shaped scar on the image and then glared at Richard. "You say this man is your boss?" he asked.

Richard nodded.

Detective Russell rose abruptly and turned the tape recorder off. He took Richard's cell phone and told him to wait. The smiling photo of Matt Gibson was still visible, as the detective disappeared down the corridor with the phone grasped in his hand.

Richard gulped all the water from the cup with a shaking hand, sloshing some down his shirt. He hoped he was doing the right thing. Judging by Detective Russell's reaction to the picture of Matt, he knew the man believed him. He really could not imagine why no one had called Matt's name in to the tip-line. Later, he found out that two people had. The messages just had not been heard yet. There were hundreds of calls, and not enough officers to listen to them all.

Russell returned with a second man. He was introduced as Special Agent Morris with the state bureau of investigation.

The tape recorder was turned back on, and Richard's water cup refilled. Hundreds of questions were fired off. Once, the special agent even asked if Richard was an accomplice and decided to turn in his boss because the guilt was too much to bear.

Richard exploded at this accusation and rose to leave. Both detectives hastily apologized, but that didn't stop them from keeping the paper cup he had drank from. While they did not consider Richard a suspect, you just never knew when you might want to run someone's DNA, should new evidence come to light.

The police had withheld certain information from the public. No match to the DNA swabs taken from the victims had been found in the national database, for instance. Another undisclosed fact was that the murderer always cut a piece of his victim's hair off to take with him as a memento.

It was nearly midnight before Richard was allowed to go home. The two detectives drove to Matt's house and hauled him in for questioning, barely giving him enough time to get dressed. As his alarmed wife watched in horror, Matt was shoved into the back of a police car. She ran inside and tearfully called her parents.

Her father located a lawyer. The disheveled barrister, with his hair still standing in wild disarray from sleep, arrived at the police department and an intense interrogation began.

Matt did not know how many hours passed, or how many times the stranger to his left enlisted by his father-in-law to defend him barked, "Don't answer that."

It took nearly an hour for Matt to fully understand what these men thought him guilty of, and he was horrified. He tried to offer DNA samples and agree to a polygraph, but the lawyer would have none of it. He kept interrupting and telling him he would do no such thing without a court order.

"What evidence do you have against Mr. Gibson, boys?" the lawyer barked.

The detectives assured him they only wanted to ask a few questions, that was all.

The attorney responded stubbornly, "Charge him or send him home. You know the rules."

Matt thought his lawyer was making him look even guiltier. He asked for a moment alone with his counsel.

"Listen, Mr…" he couldn't remember the guy's name.

"Conrad. Martin Conrad."

"Mr. Conrad, I have nothing to do with those murders. I'll give them DNA and take their lie detector test. I want to do everything in my power to show them they have the wrong guy here. You act like you think I committed those awful crimes. You are making me look guilty."

The attorney sighed and proceeded to fill Matt in on the facts of life. "Your wife's father asked me to defend you, and that's exactly what I'm doing. You need to understand something. When two homicide detectives haul you in for questioning in the middle of the night, it doesn't matter what I think. It matters what they do—and those boys think you are guilty as hell. They're convinced you are the Oceanside Strangler. And let me guess, your only alibi for the nights those crimes were committed is your wife, am I right?"

Matt nodded miserably.

"I don't think you realize how much trouble you might be in," Conrad continued. "Guilty or not, you could still end up convicted if this goes to trial and they have enough circumstantial evidence. So, before you go offering up blood samples, why don't you let me find out what they've got. Even if you are innocent, convincing a jury of twelve of your peers isn't as easy as you might think. Sometimes truthful people fail polygraphs, Matt. Sometimes innocent people go to prison. Do you understand me?"

Visibly shaken, Matt nodded.

The officers returned and Conrad informed them his client would answer only such questions as he deemed appropriate.

They reluctantly began a much less vigorous interrogation than they had originally hoped to. The questions Matt was allowed to answer were about his whereabouts on the nights the crimes were committed, and who could verify his alibi.

Matt was also asked about his relationship to all of the deceased. His vehement answer was that he never met any of them, and had no idea how he ended up being a suspect at all.

They did not tell him. Protecting their source, Richard Freeman's name was never mentioned.

The detectives asked Matt if he would be willing to stand in a police line-up. They wanted to see if the victim who had managed to escape the Oceanside Strangler could identify him.

The lawyer roared his objection and asked them again what evidence they had against his client. The police line-up request was tabled for the time being.

As dawn was breaking, they let Matt go home. While they did not have enough evidence to charge him, they showed him the police artist's rendering of the suspect. His stomach dropped when he saw the eerie resemblance to himself. He self-consciously ran a shaking hand over his chick-magnet scar.

As Matt and his attorney were leaving, Conrad held out his hand. "The soda can Mr. Gibson drank from please."

Detective Russell grudgingly handed it over. Tomorrow he would show the victim Matt's photograph. If they could get a positive ID from her, the DA might let them make an arrest. At the very least it would be probable cause to obtain a warrant for Gibson's DNA.

Russell would have preferred to pull the DNA from the soda can left behind, but Matt's lawyer had dashed that dream away with his outstretched hand.

While Matt's name was not released to the media as a person of interest due to the nasty lawsuit they knew Martin Conrad would file, they did report publicly that there were new leads and they were close to making an arrest.

Richard was even paler than usual when he arrived at work the following day. He immediately looked toward his boss's office. He was relieved to see it dark and unoccupied. Richard was certain Matt had finally been arrested.

Detective Russell showed the victim Matt's photograph. "Well," she said, "it looks kind of like him, but I'm not sure. It was awfully dark out, and the whole thing happened so fast."

The DA said no arrest. Worse, no warrant for Gibson's DNA.

The detectives decided to take matters into their own hands and installed a GPS tracking device in the wheel-well of Matt's Porsche. They had him under surveillance twenty-four seven. It didn't take long to obtain his DNA from a discarded plastic spoon when he took his children for ice cream.

Matt saw the unmarked police vehicles show up everywhere he went. They were constantly parked outside his home. He made no effort to hide from them.

For three days after they turned the plastic spoon over to the lab for DNA testing, the detectives held their breath waiting for the results. They were ready to take Matt Gibson into custody the moment they opened the envelope.

When the results came in at last, Russell raised it triumphantly over his head. "This is it!" he cried, savagely tearing open the envelope.

He nearly fainted when the results declared Gibson's DNA no match to any of the samples taken from the victims. Certain this was a mistake, Russell ordered another test. It came back negative a second time. In frustration he sent the sample to a different lab, which returned a final crushing confirmation. Had there been anything left of Matt Gibson's DNA sample to test, Russell would have happily sent it off to another lab, so convinced was he of the man's guilt. But the sample had been tested down to the last molecule, and three times it confirmed Matt Gibson was not the Oceanside Strangler.

Back at square one, both detectives were inconsolable. The district attorney ordered the GPS device removed from Matt's car.

The unmarked vehicles Matt had seen at every corner disappeared just as suddenly as they'd shown up in his life.

Conrad called him with the good news that the police no longer considered him a person of interest in the case. Though, this wasn't entirely true.

Summer gave way to autumn, and the Santa Ana winds blew in stormy weather. The murders stopped as the temperature dropped and the days grew damp and blustery. The detectives continued the exhaustive search for the Oceanside Strangler. In their hearts they still believed Matt Gibson had gotten away with murder. It was that scar. It was too unique for there to ever be another one like it. The victim described it in perfect detail; a question mark at the corner of his mouth. DNA be damned, they were convinced Matt was their man. Attorney Conrad made it clear if they harassed his client further, lawsuits would be filed. So, grudgingly, they left him alone.

Eventually life returned to normal. Matt never discovered who put the police on his tail. He remained blissfully unaware that a black cloud of suspicion still swirled about him.

Richard envied Matt all the more for having gotten away with murder. Like the detectives, despite the fact that the killings seemed to have stopped, he was convinced of Gibson's guilt.

When the weather turned cold, Richard noticed Matt owned a new pair of leather driving gloves with the Porsche logo smartly embroidered at the cuffs. He envied those, too.

Richard dusted off his online dating profile and put his angst over Denise behind him. He tried his luck again, and met a lady whose prospects for finding love seemed almost as bleak as his own.

Annalisa Sanchez was wide in the hip, small in the bosom, and made her very modest living by cleaning houses. Unlike Denise, she wasn't saving herself for Mr. Right. She fell into bed with Richard on their second date, and within a month the two were making plans to move in together.

Richard would give up his apartment and live in the small house Annalisa had inherited from her grandmother.

Richard had not quite finished packing up his apartment on the day he was to move out. Annalisa offered to take care of the last of it while he was at work.

As she began packing up Richard's bedroom closet, she reached to the top shelf to pull down a box. It was just a little too far back and out of reach. Using an umbrella to guide it forward, Annalisa over-maneuvered and the box tumbled to the floor at her feet, spilling the contents.

With a puzzled frown she picked up the strewn items from the floor. There was a dark curly wig, a pair of driving gloves with the Porsche logo embroidered on the cuffs, a receipt from a store called Midway Costume Shop, and another from The Wig Palace.

There was also a package of strange gummy looking rubber pieces in different sizes and shapes. The package read:

WARTS, MOLES AND SCARS
***A HALLOWEEN MUST HAVE ***
SOLD EXCLUSIVELY BY MIDWAY

With a mew of disgust, Annalisa dropped the package. She froze when she saw the final item from the box lying against her foot. With numb fingers she picked up a plastic sandwich bag with a zip-lock closure. Inside were nine small bundles of long hair, each secured with a bobby pin. Her bobby pins!

Flinging the bag away like it was hot, Annalisa stumbled from the closet. With vivid clarity, she remembered Richard saying how badly he struggled with his conscience before turning in his boss to the authorities because he was convinced Matt Gibson was the Oceanside Strangler. It was the police sketch that had convinced him. Matt Gibson had the same scar, the same mole and the same curly hair as the suspect.

Annalisa's mind frantically searched for some logical explanation for the incriminating items unearthed in Richard's closet. There was none.

She donned a pair of kitchen gloves and hastily dropped the items back into the box. She fought an overwhelming wave of nausea as she gingerly lay the baggy containing the hair-clippings of nine murdered women on top.

Annalisa ran out of the apartment and out of Richard Freeman's life.

As she entered the police department Annalisa began to swoon. Concerned, an officer rushed to her side.

"Ma'am, are you alright?"

She thrust the box into his hands and started sobbing.

"What's this?" he asked, beginning to open the top.

"That's the Oceanside Strangler," she stammered, and slipped to the floor in a dead faint.

The officer eyed the box apprehensively as he summoned paramedics. He would let Pete Russell deal with it.

Half an hour later, Annalisa sat sipping a steaming cup of tea in the same airless room where both Matt Gibson, and her boy-friend, Richard Freeman—aka the Oceanside Strangler—had sat before her.

Lieutenant Russell and Special Agent Morris listened to her recount the story of packing up Richard's closet for his move to her house, and the box sliding off the shelf and revealing the horrors within.

They exchanged a look of utter disbelief, mingled with deep shame. The Oceanside Strangler had been right under their noses. It occurred to both detectives at the same moment, that had Annalisa not found that box, they would never have solved those dreadful crimes. Worse, Annalisa Sanchez may have very well turned out to be another victim, and it would be entirely their fault. They could hardly meet the lady's eyes. One DNA test on a paper cup still sitting in Russel's desk and this would have been over months ago.

When Richard arrived home he saw an open moving box sitting in his bedroom. Annalisa had clearly begun packing up his closet, but she had not finished. Richard wondered where she was.

When the knock at the door came, Richard navigated his way around the sea of boxes, calling, "Anna? Did you forget your key?"

His eyes widened in surprise when he opened the door. "Detectives!" he cried, a broad smile lighting his face. "What brings you here? Did you catch the Oceanside Strangler?"

Russell looked at Morris and shook his head. "Yes, Mr. Freeman, I believe we did," he replied.

According to the battery of psychiatrists enlisted by the court to examine Richard, he suffered some type of psychotic break after Denise left him. He envied Matt Gibson so much that he wanted to become him. And he hated Denise so much for breaking his heart that he wanted to kill her. Over and over again. He was deemed incapable of standing trial and remanded to a mental institution for the criminally insane.

Even after extensive psychological treatment and powerful anti-psychotic medications, Richard still refused to believe he was the Oceanside Strangler. He insisted they had the wrong man. It was Matt Gibson who should be locked up, not him.

After it was all over, the detectives paid Matt a visit. They offered what apologies they could. Matt told them he understood they were just doing their job.

His wife was not nearly so gracious. She told them they should be ashamed of themselves before stomping from the room.

The detectives felt much the same way.

Matt shook his head and looked terribly sad when he said he had no idea Richard Freeman was mentally ill.

The detectives confided that even as seasoned detectives, they had not figured it out either. Richard had hidden the truth from everyone, including himself.

As they were leaving, Russell stopped at the bottom of the porch steps. "Oh, I almost forgot." He pulled Matt's driving gloves from his pocket. "I believe these are yours. Freeman won't admit to killing those women, but he did admit to stealing these from you."

Matt held up his hands and grimaced. "I don't want them anymore. Please just throw them away."

The detectives stared transfixed at Matt's scowl. It had momentarily stretched his oddly shaped scar, transforming it from a question mark into an exclamation point. It appeared like an omen. A final, violent punctuation mark on the nasty business just concluded.

LET SLEEPING CATS LIE

Spring 1979

WHEN LEANNE SIMS nine year-old daughter, Jillian, appeared in the kitchen holding a frail kitten protectively in her arms, Leanne knew almost verbatim the conversation that was about to take place. It was one she had shared with her daughter many times, nearly since the day the little girl had learned to walk.

First would come the explanation of where the stray animal had been found, followed by the same question: "Mom, can we keep it?"

Leanne's daughter had a very tender heart toward every living thing. Spiders were not allowed to be killed. They had to be gently escorted outside. The child kept a supply of fresh plant leaves in the garage just in case the hibernating pair of snails that one day appeared stuck to the back wall in there should wake up hungry. The snails had been up there for three years. Leanne was pretty certain they were dead, and all that remained were empty shells, but neither she nor her husband had the heart to tell Jillian.

The child began leaving bowls of cat food outside the house from the time she could reach the bag containing the kibble. This produced a rash of strays flocking to their home, and a costly and exhausting seven year mission of spaying, neutering and finding homes for over five dozen cats before the stray population in their neighborhood was finally under control. Currently the Sims household owned six cats and four dogs, all strays brought home by Jillian.

Leanne took the small kitten from her daughter's arms. It was clearly malnourished. She sighed, producing a bowl from under the sink to feed the little thing.

"Okay, honey, I will ask your father when he gets home tonight. But, I'm telling you, this will have to be the last one. It's a wonder your dad hasn't thrown us both out."

She worried about Jillian a great deal when she envisioned the child's future. She pictured a home over-run with stray animals. Leanne did not believe her little girl would ever out-grow her soft heart, or be able to turn her back on any animal in need. Jillian was on a mission to save the world, and she was doing it one cat at a time. It scared Leanne when she thought about what lie ahead for Jillian. She didn't like to think of her youngest daughter growing up to be known as "The Crazy Cat Lady."

Summer 2005

Jillian Oliver pulled into her driveway and popped the trunk latch on her late model Buick. She began to pull the grocery bags out just as her neighbor, Lois Ross, stalked across the front lawn to confront her.

Jillian pasted a small, polite smile, devoid of any real sincerity onto her face, as she dropped the bag she was holding back into the car and turned to face the angry, overweight woman approaching.

"Good morning, Lois," Jillian said through gritted teeth.

Skipping the pleasantries, the woman barked in a shower of spittle, "Your cat tore up my tulips again. How many times do I have to tell you to keep him out of my garden?"

There was a laundry list of grievances Lois Ross had against the Oliver family pets. In Jillian's mind, tearing up the tulips was number five on the list. It came right after number four; *the dogs bark late at night and wake me up*, and just before *your cat tried to attack me.* Though, no evidence of any such attack had ever been visible anywhere on the unpleasant woman's body.

Insincere smile still firmly in place, Jillian responded, "I would be happy to replant the tulips for you, Lois. Just let me get my groceries put up."

Knowing full well no torn up tulips would be produced, Jillian waited for her neighbor's reply.

Lois glared at Jillian through small, glinting piglet eyes, which lay nestled within about an acre of doughy, pale flesh. She spat, "I don't want you to replant my flowers. I want you to keep that damn cat of yours inside the house and away from my yard. If you don't, I swear I will call the pound." With that she turned on her heel and stalked back into her house, slamming the door behind her.

Jillian's smiling face settled into a worried frown. It was one she would wear for the rest of the day, and one her husband would instantly recognize when he arrived home from work that evening.

While, so far, the irritating woman had not made good on her threat to call the pound, Jillian lived in constant fear that one day they would show up on her doorstep, and she wouldn't have time to hide the six furry felines residing inside.

The county allowed for three animals per household. The Oliver family met that quota with their dogs alone. Lois did not know exactly how many pets Jillian owned, but she knew it was a hell of a lot more than three. The one she complained about today was Crayon, a three year old Calico who went crazy when locked indoors. Crayon found creative ways to sneak out on a daily basis, despite Jillian's attempts to keep him indoors. He was the only one of the cats who ever escaped, and once, he had indeed gone into Lois Ross's yard and done some digging. From that day on all hell had broken loose.

Jillian and her husband Scott were once on better terms with Lois Ross. This was before their four-legged menagerie had grown to its current numbers, and they were still within the legal limit.

The real trouble started one Christmas a few years back when they had invited Lois and Neil Ross to a holiday party at their home. Neil got drunk and made a sloppy pass at Jillian. She politely deflected it, but later that evening when she told her husband about the incident, he had gone next door and confronted Neil. The two men had a heated argument and Lois blatantly called Jillian a liar. Scott had the good sense to leave before the confrontation escalated to blows. Ever since then, things were never the same. Over time the situation steadily eroded, and Lois Ross began taking every opportunity which presented itself to make Jillian's life a living hell. Her dislike of the Oliver family pets was really just a symptom of a much larger problem.

Both Jillian and her husband knew Lois was extremely insecure and very jealous of Jillian's slim body. Even after giving birth to three children she still maintained the figure she sported in her twenties. Lois, on the other hand, was childless and had struggled with her weight since high school. She was now bordering on obesity. She saw the way her husband looked at Jillian and she didn't like it one bit.

The next assault from Lois Ross came in the form of a midnight phone call ordering Jillian and Scott to silence the barking dogs. The problem with this was that the dogs were not barking. Ten minutes before, Scott had let the dogs in the backyard for a final potty break before bed. Snowball, their Malamute, barked once before the dogs were ushered back inside. Only once. Scott pointed this out to Lois on the phone, who promptly voiced another threat to call the pound before hanging up.

Lois was a known insomniac. It was not uncommon for her to go out in the middle of the night. Her destination was usually the Indian Casino a few miles away, where she would play slot machines until after sunrise. She seemed like a miserable and tortured woman to Jillian, who had initially tried to befriend her. This was before Lois accused Jillian of lying when her husband groped her, and before her constant verbal assaults began on the Oliver family pets.

The situation seemed to be escalating and Jillian was unsure why. Something had once again put a bee in Lois Ross's bonnet, and Jillian had no idea what set her off again.

One evening when Scott was working late, Jillian put the kids to bed and poured a glass of wine. She carried it out to the backyard and sat on a lounge chair by edge of their pool to enjoy the mild California evening. A few minutes later, Neil Ross poked his head over the fence.

"Well, hey there, Jilly. How's tricks?" He was grinning like a loon.

Jillian wondered, *Do people really talk like that anymore?* She hated being called Jill and absolutely no one had ever called her Jilly. Her neighbor was kind of creepy. He had begun making Jillian nervous long before the ridiculous incident at their Christmas party.

"Evening, Neil," Jillian responded politely.

"Where's Scott tonight?"

Jillian grimaced. "Oh, he's on his way home now. Had to work late."

Neil barked a lecherous laugh, "Ah, the old working late excuse, huh? Wink, wink, nod, nod."

When he saw a look of disgust cross his pretty neighbor's face he changed the subject at once.

Clearing his throat, Neil said, "Listen, Jill. Lois is pretty upset about the cat digging in our yard again. It would really be better if you kept it inside."

Exasperated, Jillian replied, "Oh, for Pete's sake! The cat hasn't gotten out in days. I have no idea what Lois is so upset about, but it's not Crayon's fault." She rose from the lounge chair and picked up her still full wine glass. She didn't want it anymore.

"Well, I'm just giving you fair warning. Lois isn't happy with you. She's making noise about calling Animal Control again."

Tears brimming in Jillian's eyes, she bid Neil Ross a hasty goodnight, and went back inside.

When Scott arrived home, Jillian relayed the conversation with the neighbor to him. He put his arm around his wife and comforted her as best he could. He knew Jillian was upset, and did not want to add to her angst, but he had a bad feeling about their neighbor and they needed to be prepared in the event Lois made good on her threat.

"Honey," Scott said, "Have you thought about what you are going to do if she does call the pound?"

Jillian's eyes flew open in fear, "Oh, Scott, do you really think she will? She doesn't actually know how many pets we have. All she has ever seen is Crayon and the dogs."

"You don't know that. The cats sit in the windows, and I swear that woman spies on us. She may not know the exact number, but she knows it's more than three. We need a plan just in case."

"As much as I hate to lock them up, maybe during the day I ought to keep the cats in the den for a while. Just until this latest assault blows over."

Her husband was thoughtful for a moment. "What if they want to look through the house?"

"Scott, are you trying to frighten me?"

"No, babe. I just don't want any trouble."

Jillian sighed. "I don't want to talk about this anymore tonight. I'll figure something out."

Scott hoped that was true. He knew his wife, and she would sweep it under the rug until she was forced to deal with it. He hoped that day would not come, but his gut told him it would. And not long after, it did.

Jillian was folding clothes when she glanced out the window and saw a truck parked at the curb. It was from Animal Control. She dropped the blouse she was holding and darted down the hallway to her oldest daughter, Karen's, bedroom. She tapped urgently on the door. "Sweetie, come out here please. I need your help. Now!"

Her daughter flung the door open. Seeing her mother's worried expression Karen sprang into action. Only ten years old, but wise beyond her years, Karen asked, "The pound?"

Jillian nodded, and together they headed for the den, where all six cats lay sleeping.

Jillian instructed Karen to carry all the cats into the bathroom and turn on the water in the shower. She was to lock herself in there with the cats until the Animal Control officer was gone.

While Karen transferred the cats into the bathroom, Jillian swept up the few stray pieces of cat litter from the floor and stowed the litter box, food bowls, and all telltale signs of a cat in residence into the closet. For good measure she sprayed a healthy shot of air freshener into the room.

When she looked out the front window, she could see Lois Ross speaking to the man from animal control. Meaty arms flying, chubby hands gesturing wildly, she was pointing an accusatory finger in the direction of Jillian's house. The man in the khaki uniform was nodding and taking notes.

A few moments later he strode to the front door and rang the bell. Jillian smoothed her hair, and did her best to arrange her face into a look of casual disinterest as she opened the door.

"Can I help you?" she asked. She was relieved to hear her voice sounded steady.

"Good afternoon, ma'am. I am with Los Angeles County Animal Control," he said, producing a business card and handing it to Jillian. "We have received a complaint from one of your neighbors."

Jillian glanced at the card. "What kind of complaint?"

"She claims you have more than a dozen animals here. The county allows for a maximum of three pets per household. I would like to take a look inside if you don't mind."

Jillian laughed like the idea was ludicrous and opened the door wider to allow the man entry. "I'm afraid Mrs. Ross and I have had some issues in the past. I think this is just her way of harassing me."

Stepping into the foyer he put his nose in the air like a horse sensing fire and gave a loud sniff.

Jillian closed her eyes and fought to slow down her rapidly pounding heart. She kept the litter boxes fastidiously clean, and didn't think there were any obvious signs of the felines, but she didn't know just how sensitive this trained officer's nose was either. She prayed silently that she hadn't left a stray catnip toy lying anywhere in plain sight.

"Well, nonetheless, I will just have a quick look around, and then I will get out of your hair."

Jillian led the officer through the house. She stopped in the upstairs hallway before the bathroom and said, "My daughter is taking a shower, so you can't go in there, but you can look in the bedrooms if you would like."

Once he had completed the walkthrough, he asked Jillian, "Do you have any cats? The neighbor said one has torn up her garden."

Without hesitation, Jillian replied, "We used to. Now we just have the dogs."

"And are they licensed and vaccinated?"

"Of course. I will show you the paperwork. It's downstairs."

Five minutes later the officer apologized for the inconvenience and left. His report would say there was no evidence of any cats. It noted there were three dogs, all with the appropriate proof that they were properly licensed and vaccinated.

Jillian breathed a huge sigh of relief when the man left and hurried to let her daughter and the cats out of the bathroom.

After that incident, for a while things were better. Lois Ross stayed mostly out of Jillian's way and there were no more surprise visits from the pound. Gradually Jillian stopped jumping every time the doorbell rang.

Early the following year Jillian's daughter told her mother of a stray cat she kept seeing near her school. Jillian located the cat, and one afternoon when she picked up her daughter she picked up the cat, too. Though she tried to place it in a shelter, all the no-kill ones were full, so the Oliver family adopted it. Her six year old son, Troy, named the little white newcomer Binky. It was discovered that Binky was declawed. Jillian would have happily strangled whoever declawed a cat and then left it outside to fend for itself. Binky brought the Oliver pet total to ten now.

Scott needed to go to Las Vegas on business. He thought it would be a nice break for Jillian if she could accompany him on the trip. At first she balked, saying, "Oh, hon. I don't know. Who would take care of the kids and the critters?"

Scott suggested Jillian ask her sister, Shelby, if she could come stay with the kids. Shelby adored her nieces and nephew and readily agreed to babysit the children and see after the pets. Jillian was ecstatic to have a mini-vacation with her husband.

While Scott and Jillian were away, things were quiet in the Oliver household until the third and final evening of their trip. Shelby and the kids were in the living room watching a movie. Karen and her sister, Beth, went to the kitchen to get everyone drinks. On their way there they were absolutely stunned to see Mrs. Ross standing in their backyard. Her bulk was pressed up against the dining room window, and she was snapping pictures on her cell phone through the glass. It was a lovely sunny day, with the sun just beginning to sink behind the mountains. Five of the seven cats in residence were clearly in view through the window. All were stretched out and dozing, enjoying the warmth of the slanting bars of lingering sunlight shining through the skylights and side windows of the house.

Karen gasped. Thinking quickly, she ran and drew the curtains closed. "Aunt Shelby," she cried. "Please come in here."

Hearing the alarm in her niece's voice, Shelby hurried into the dining room. When Karen explained what they had just witnessed, Shelby marched into the backyard prepared to do battle with the woman. By the time she reached the door, Lois Ross had retreated back to the safety of her own nest. Shelby decided not to knock on the neighbor's door and pursue any confrontation. She knew the trouble her sister had been going through with the awful woman and did not want to make the situation any worse than it already was.

Karen asked, "Should we call Mom and Dad?"

Shelby thought about it for a moment before replying, "No. Let's not spoil their trip. We'll tell them about it when they get home tomorrow."

Later that night, after the kids were asleep and Shelby had seen the dogs out to the backyard for their last potty break of the evening, she locked all the doors.

Spooning some cat food into bowls in the kitchen for a little late night snack, she called to her wards. The previous night, as soon as they heard the pop tops on the food cans, all seven cats charged into the kitchen for their treat. Oddly, tonight, only the newcomer, Binky, ran into the kitchen. Shelby put the bowls down on the floor and went searching for the others. When she had put Troy to bed, Gemma, a beautiful marmalade colored tabby, jumped on the bed with him and promptly fell asleep next to his pillow, so perhaps she was still in his room. However, when Shelby checked all the bedrooms, looked under every bed and behind every piece of furniture, she grew alarmed. Where on earth could six cats be hiding? And for that matter, why? They were normally all in plain sight, and they never missed a chance to have a little snack. So, where were they?

When an hour passed, Shelby was worried enough to call her boyfriend and wake him up to come help her search for the missing felines.

Around midnight, just as she was getting frantic, Shelby watched as the irritable neighbor lady backed out of her driveway and left home. She wondered where she was going this late.

Shelby and her boyfriend, Walt, scoured the neighborhood and surrounding blocks until after two o'clock in the morning before they gave up their search.

Shelby was beside herself. Not only was she going to have to tell her sister about the neighbor trespassing and snapping pictures of the cats, she was also going to have to tell her that somehow she managed to lose six of her beloved pets. How the hell did they get out?

Jillian had warned her repeatedly about Crayon being a known flight risk and an accomplished escape artist. She had been so careful to make sure the doors and windows were always closed. How could six cats just vanish like that?

Exhausted and worried, Shelby and Walt fell into a troubled doze on the sofa. Just before dawn they were awakened by an insistent scratching at the back door. The two cautiously approached the window facing onto the back patio. They were stunned to see all six missing cats huddled there, scratching at the door and meowing to be let in. Shelby and Walt exchanged a puzzled, but relieved look, as she flung the door open and ushered the felines inside. Neither one noticed the bloody paw prints tattooed on the patio and door where the kitties had requested entry after their late-night sojourn.

Walt said, "I didn't know cats travelled in packs. That was weird."

Shelby nodded her agreement. "Very. Do you think I even need to tell Jillian about this? I mean they are all back, and no harm done, right?"

Walt shook his head. "Naw. Why tell her? She might get mad at you."

Shelby didn't think Jillian would be angry with her, but she might not ever trust her to look after things again when she and Scott went away. None of the kids were awake or knew what had happened, and all felines were back and accounted for. Shelby decided to keep it to herself. It was going to be hard enough telling Jillian about Lois Ross's latest stunt with the camera. The fact that the cats had gone missing was one detail Jillian definitely didn't need to learn about.

On her way back to bed Shelby scooped up Binky and kissed his clawless toes. "You were the only good one in the bunch," she cooed to the kitten. "Guess you're a lover, not a leaver, huh baby?"

Scott, Jillian and Shelby sat around the kitchen table drinking coffee and discussing Lois Ross. Jillian and Scott were both clearly worried about the photographs. Now the Ross woman would have proof that they were well over the county sanctioned number of three pets, and they had no idea what to do. They did not know what the miserable woman was planning on doing with those pictures, but knew it sure wasn't entering the cats in a world's cutest kitty contest. Jillian wondered how many times the "My daughter is taking a shower" ruse would work on a suspicious Animal Control officer. She had a feeling that was a one shot deal.

At best they would be leveled with a hefty fine and ordered to reduce the number of animals they were housing. At worst, a team of officers in khaki uniforms would show up and take away their cats. This was terrible.

Shelby felt responsible and offered to take the cats to her apartment. Unfortunately her roommate was deathly allergic, so it was completely out of the question. Scott and Jillian did their best to reassure Shelby that none of this was her fault, but they could see how awfully guilty she was feeling. Neither had any idea that much of her guilt was not entirely over Lois Ross's unauthorized photo shoot. Shelby still could not quite forgive herself for misplacing six of her sister's pets for several hours the previous night.

With no idea what to do about Lois Ross, and no idea who the photos she had taken were being seen by, Scott and Jillian thanked Shelby for taking care of things while they were away and sent her home.

About an hour before the kids were due home from school Scott went to the grocery store to pick up something for dinner.

Jillian went outside to water the plants. She had just turned the hose on when a tall man in a dark suit appeared standing in her driveway. Her heart sped up and her hands grew clammy. While this man was not wearing the telltale khaki uniform of Animal Control, he certainly had an official air about him. Jillian turned off the hose and wiped her hands on the back of her jeans.

The man looked pleasant enough as he approached with his hand extended. "Hello there. Are you Mrs. Oliver?"

Jillian nodded and shook the offered hand. "Yes. And who might you be?"

He reached into the breast pocket of his jacket and took out a small leather case. He opened it for Jillian's inspection. It contained a badge and an ID card from the Los Angeles police department. "My name is Detective Hanson. I'm with the homicide division for the LAPD."

Homicide? Jillian thought, and oddly felt some relief. This visit clearly wasn't about her cats.

"Uh oh, who died?" she asked.

The detective studied her closely for a moment before answering. "How friendly are you with your neighbor, Mrs. Ross?" he asked.

Jillian offered a small chilly smile. "Friendly? We are not friendly at all, Detective. Did Lois kill somebody?"

Again the detective observed her carefully. Jillian waited patiently for him to answer her question. He didn't. Instead he asked, "I'd like to ask you some questions if you don't mind. Can we go inside?"

Jillian shook her head regretfully. "I'd rather not. Let's just speak out here."

After another pause, the detective nodded. "I understand from Mrs. Ross's husband that you and she had a long standing grudge. Is that true?"

"She has the grudge. In fact, she hates me."

"And how do you feel about her?"

Jillian shrugged, and said simply, "I just wish she would leave me alone."

"Mr. Ross says you tried to irritate her on purpose. Something about sending your cats into her garden. Is that true?"

Jillian rolled her eyes. "Oh, Mr. Ross says that, does he? In case you didn't notice, Mr. Ross is a bit of a creep."

"I take it you don't much like him any more than you do his wife," the detective observed.

"I liked him much better before he grabbed my ass at a party a few years back," Jillian replied dryly.

Yeah, Hanson could see that. The guy definitely struck him as an ass grabber. He emitted this weird vibe that reminded Hanson of the 1970's disco hoppers; long sideburns, blow-dried hair, white John Travolta polyester suit, and an unbuttoned shirt, complete with several gold chains nestled in the exposed chest hair. While that wasn't what Neil Ross actually looked like now, he still somehow reeked of it.

A picture was emerging in Hanson's mind of the neighbors' relationship. The wife was jealous of the pretty lady next door with the pleasing figure, and the husband was pissed off at the same neighbor because she had rejected his advances.

He asked Jillian, "Where were you last night, around, oh, say one or two o'clock in the morning?"

Jillian replied, "I was in Las Vegas with my husband. We returned home this morning. Our plane landed around eleven-thirty."

The detective realized that was a pretty airtight alibi and could be easily verified. He was starting to think this woman was probably not his suspect after all. He decided to come clean with her and see if she could shed some light on this strange case.

"Mrs. Oliver, Lois Ross was found dead in her car early this morning."

Jillian's hand flew to her chest. She cried, "Oh my god! What happened?"

From the description the victim's husband had given him of Jillian Oliver, Detective Hanson came prepared to meet a woman who would dodge his questions, act evasive and behave as though she was guilty of something. He was completely disarmed by this woman's candor. She was clearly not hiding anything, and he had been a homicide detective long enough to know the death of her neighbor had just taken her completely by surprise. There was not a single thing in her body language to suggest any guilt, or even any knowledge of the crime.

"She was... well, I don't really know how else to say this, but it looks like she was mauled, or more accurately, ripped to death by something. Something like cats. There was, in fact, some cat hair found in the car and on her clothing.

"Cats? Housecats?" Jillian asked incredulously.

The detective nodded.

Jillian laughed a dry, humorless chuckle. "Detective Hanson, Mrs. Ross is a... uh... formidable woman. I honestly can't think of any cat, with the exception of a mountain lion, the woman couldn't fend off. Can you?"

The detective shrugged. "Well, we don't have any mountain lions in the San Fernando Valley, so I don't know what got at her, but something sure did. She's covered in hundreds of scratches and her hands were torn to shreds fighting off whatever it was. It wasn't a pretty scene."

Jillian visibly paled and the detective apologized. "Sorry, Mrs. Oliver. Guess that was a little too much information."

Jillian shook her head sadly. "Is there anything else, Detective?"

"Just a few more questions. Were you aware that Mrs. Ross took pictures of your cats yesterday? According to her husband she was planning on filing a formal complaint against you with both Animal Control and the Board of Health."

"My daughters saw her in our backyard. I had no idea what she was planning on doing with the photos, however."

"How many cats do you have?"

When Jillian hesitated, the detective hastily added, "Don't worry, I'm not here to get you into any trouble, I just want to solve this thing."

Jillian sighed. "I have seven cats. They were all rescues."

Detective Hanson thought about Terrence, his bull dog. Terrence had been living with a couple that left him chained to a fence with no shelter, every day, and in all seasons. The dog had nothing to lie on but the cold cement. Detective Hanson became aware of the dog's plight through some fellow officers who had been called out to the home three times on domestic violence complaints. He wanted to get the dog out of there, but could think of no legal channels which would have placed the dog in any better circumstances. The local animal shelter was a dismal and awful place. It was hard enough for puppies to get adopted, let alone a six-year-old dog with hip dysplasia.

Being a cop, he couldn't just go kidnap the poor thing… but his friend, and fellow dog lover, Cody, had no such reservations. On a drizzly Tuesday afternoon when they were both at work,

Cody marched into the couple's backyard armed with a leash and a hotdog. He fed the dog the hotdog and unchained him. Cody walked the dog out of the yard like he had every right to be there, even stopping at the curb to allow the pooch to relieve himself. Terrence had been living with Detective Hanson ever since. He could appreciate Mrs. Oliver's situation, and actually thought the world of the lady for taking in so many homeless animals.

He had read the Animal Control report and knew the house was well kept and clean. Being quite a bit more savvy than an animal control officer, Hanson also knew exactly where the cats were hidden during the inspection. It said in the report that the officer had seen every room in the house except a bathroom where someone was said to be showering. He had to hand it to Mrs. Oliver. She was no dummy.

She was no killer either. He smiled and nodded when she finally invited him inside for a cup of coffee.

Once they were settled at the kitchen table, Binky jumped in the detective's lap and curled up in a ball. He lay contentedly purring while the detective stroked his head.

"Do you know of anyone else the Ross woman was having trouble with?" Detective Hanson asked while sipping his coffee.

Jillian shook her head. "Sorry, I don't. She was a very unpleasant person, however, so I am sure I am not the only one she had grievances with." She hesitated for a moment, and then said, "Now, may I ask you a question, Detective?"

"Sure."

"What do you think mauled her? I mean really. I know you don't believe it was a housecat." She pointed to the fluffy white kitty sprawled on the detective's knees.

Hanson shrugged. "I don't know. ME is calling it homicide, so I am investigating it as one. Honestly, I don't have a clue what got to her. Damndest thing I ever saw. It was like something out of Jurassic Park, that Michael Crichton book. Did you ever read that?"

A frown furrowed Jillian's brow. "Oh, Detective, surely you don't think it was dinosaurs that did it? That's about the only thing less likely than housecats."

"I'm just saying it is very weird," Hanson answered uncomfortably. He was finding it a little too easy talking to Mrs. Oliver, and realized he was voicing just about every notion that popped into his brain. It was time to go.

The detective rose to leave and gently placed Binky on the chair. He thanked Jillian for the coffee.

"I sure hope you have some other leads beside me," Jillian said sadly.

He told her, "Mrs. Ross was known to frequent a casino in the wee hours of the morning. That's my next stop. Maybe someone there can give me something more. Her car was found just a mile or so from the place."

"Good luck, Detective. I hope you find out what happened to her. I didn't much like her, but I certainly never wanted anything like this to happen."

As she was seeing him out, Jillian sighed. "I suppose her husband will carry on her legacy and pass along those pictures she took to the proper authorities so they can bust me."

Detective Hanson smiled and shook his head. "He can't. We took Mrs. Ross's phone. We need to examine it for evidence. I don't think you have to worry about that anymore."

Jillian offered the detective a grateful smile. The nightmare was finally over.

Spring 2010

Keller Vaughn was the LAPD's newest fair-haired boy and media hero. Transferred in to head up the cold case division, he had an unparalleled success rate in solving crimes and a distinguished history with the department. He'd risen through the ranks from patrol officer to his current position with impressive speed. He was young, energetic, smart and never let emotion cloud his judgment. He didn't really care how much he might like you. If you were guilty, he was going to prove it. His investigative techniques were not always orthodox, and once you were on his radar you never fell off. It was nearly impossible to erase the cloud of suspicion from his heart.

When the cold murder case of Lois Ross landed on his desk, Vaughn was intrigued. There was only one suspect; a pretty suburban soccer mom with too many housecats and an iron-clad alibi. Interesting.

Keller read the case file twice. He had tremendous respect for Detective Hanson, whose success rate at solving homicides was nearly as noteworthy as his own, but he could see Hanson hadn't really looked all that closely at Jillian Oliver. Maybe it was because of her indestructible alibi. Or maybe Hanson had a blind spot for the Oliver woman because she was an animal lover, like himself. It was possible.

Keller had put away plenty of guilty people who went to great pains to set up their alibis before committing unspeakable crimes. You only had to watch Dateline to see that type of thing happened all the time. Keller Vaughn, however, didn't watch Dateline—he was the person who Dateline called requesting interviews. He broke the unbreakable, and stopped killers from getting away with murder.

Vaughn suspected Hanson's haste in clearing Jillian as a suspect had less to do with her airtight alibi, and more to do with their shared affection for all things furry. Detective Hanson's office contained more pictures of his dog than it did his wife.

Right from the start Vaughn thought Jillian Oliver was involved in the murder of Lois Ross. Whether she was the person who had actually sliced the woman to ribbons or not, one way or another, he was convinced she was involved in the crime up to her eyeballs.

No one else had any motive, and this was a very up-close and personal crime. There was nothing random about it. If someone had followed Ross from the casino, robbery would have been the intent. The victim had been lucky at the slots that night. Her purse was found right beside her in the car with several hundred dollars in cash inside. She was still wearing her jewelry. Clearly it was not a robbery.

There was only one person in the world with any motive to kill that woman. In fact, Jillian Oliver had seven furry reasons to want Lois Ross dead.

Detective Vaughn decided to pay Mrs. Oliver a visit and take her on a little trip down memory lane. He had seen in the case file that Hanson had pulled the video surveillance from both the hotel in Las Vegas and the airport, confirming Jillian Oliver was right where she claimed to be, so Vaughn didn't need to follow up on that. The part that bothered him wasn't the lady's alibi anyway. It was the cat hairs found at the crime scene. They had never been tested against cat hairs from the Oliver home. The hairs taken from the scene were still in a plastic bag down in the evidence room. They could still be tested. The question was how was Vaughn going to get samples from Jillian's cats? No judge was going to issue a court order. Not with her zipped up alibi and not even so much as a fingerprint found anywhere near the Ross woman's body. There was not one shred of evidence except those damn cat hairs. The more he examined the photos of the injuries the victim sustained, the more convinced he was they were cat scratches. Hundreds of them.

Vaughn had seen some strange things over the years, but he had never seen anything like this. Was it possible to train cats to kill? You could do it with dogs, so who could prove that you couldn't teach cats to attack?

Maybe the sister was involved. Why had she never been questioned? There was still plenty of work to be done on this peculiar case before it could be classified as unsolvable. And Keller Vaughn would enjoy every minute of the investigation.

Jillian Oliver had just finished ferrying her children to their various activities. She was enjoying a much needed break from ballet classes, little league and cheerleading practice.

She was in the backyard reading a magazine and eating a cookie when the doorbell rang. With a sigh of disappointment, she pulled herself off the lounge chair and entered the house. When she opened the front door, she did not recognize her visitor.

The young and very attractive man reached out to shake Jillian's hand, while simultaneously reaching into the pocket of his slacks with his left hand. In a practiced move he extracted his badge and identification and thrust it under Jillian's nose. He was standing so close that he was practically right on top of her. She instantly did not like him.

"Mrs. Oliver?" he asked. His right hand tightened on hers, turning the handshake into an assault. In what looked like a complicated dance move, he maneuvered her backwards through the doorway and stepped inside the threshold.

Alarmed, Jillian tried to maneuver the intruder right back out, but he had already shut the door behind him. He was in the foyer, and clearly wasn't leaving.

Jillian took the identification the man was still shoving in her face. Glancing at it briefly, and backing up a few steps to escape his overwhelming closeness, she said, "Yes. I'm Jillian Oliver. What can I do for you, Officer Keller?"

"It's Detective—Detective Vaughn. Keller is my first name. I'd like to ask you some questions about the murder of Lois Ross. May I sit down?" Not waiting for an answer, he walked past Jillian and entered the living room, uninvited.

He moved with the oily speed of a serpent and Jillian felt like she couldn't even catch her breath.

Without warning, he picked up Crayon from the couch and rubbed the startled cat back and forth against his shirt, and then put him back down. He spotted Binky on a chair and approached the cat. Binky saw him coming, flew off the chair and dashed up the stairs before the officer could grab him.

Unperturbed, Vaughn spun around and walked into the dining room, where another cat sat in the window. Jillian was following behind the officer as he barged through the house. She was panic stricken.

Finally getting her wits about her, she yelled. "Stop! Stop right now. You were not invited in, and I want you to leave immediately."

Vaughn ignored her and lifted the cat from the window sill. He rubbed him back and forth on his clothing the same way he had rubbed Crayon. The detective was rewarded by a hiss, and claws sunk deep into his hand. Vaughn voiced a wounded cry and dropped the offended animal to the floor.

Jillian shouted, "I said stop! Don't you dare touch another one of my cats. I am telling you for the last time to get out of my house, or I will call your superiors."

Detective Vaughn held up his hands in a defensive gesture. "Take it easy, I'm going. Aren't you wondering why I paid you a visit today, though? Not even a little curious?"

Jillian didn't care one bit for the high good humor or the smugness in his voice. "You can tell me from the front porch. Please leave now."

The detective retreated toward the front door, but not before running his hand through a kitty bed lying on the floor and pulling off pieces of fur clinging to the fabric. He stuffed them in his pocket.

Jillian shrieked, "What are you doing? Don't you touch one more thing in this house, Detective. I mean it." She was shaking uncontrollably with fear and rage.

Once she finally managed to get him outside, she stepped onto the porch and closed the front door behind her. "How dare you push your way into my home…" she began.

Vaughn cut her off. "How did you do it? That's the only part I can't figure. How did you pull it off? Was it your sister? Did she help you? Shelby's my next stop after I leave here. Maybe I can get her to tell me."

Jillian stared at the man dumbstruck. "Tell you what? What are you talking about?"

Neither Jillian nor the detective noticed that all of Jillian's cats were now sitting in the window watching the tense exchange. Seven sweet, furry faces staring with fury at the man who had destroyed the tranquility of their afternoon.

Vaughn spat, "I'm talking about your neighbor, Lois Ross."

Jillian gasped. "Speak to Detective Hanson. I told him everything I know four years ago."

"Oh, but Detective Hanson liked you, didn't he, Jillian? I bet he was maybe even a little sweet on you back then, wasn't he? I think the old boy thought you were kindred spirits, or something like that."

Jillian looked at Keller Vaughn like he was crazy. It was like trying to talk to someone who didn't speak the same language. Wasn't even from the same planet.

"I think you better leave now," Jillian said. "Don't come back here again."

She went inside the house and closed the door behind her.

Vaughn yelled from the porch, "Oh, Jillian, I'll be back for sure. You can count on it. And next time I'll have an arrest warrant."

Jillian called her sister to warn her not to answer the door. She thought Keller Vaughn was a mad man. She told Shelby, "I left a message for Detective Hanson. I am hoping he can get this lunatic off our backs. I think he honestly believes I killed Lois Ross."

After finally falling into fitful slumber with the help of a sleeping tablet, Jillian was awakened by a chorus of meowing and the sound of scratching at the back door. She looked to see if the racket had awakened Scott, but he slept on, snoring softly under the covers with Binky asleep on his chest. The glowing numerals on the clock read 4:16 AM.

Jillian rose from bed and went downstairs to investigate the racket. Her heart began fluttering in her chest when she saw who was on the back porch demanding entry into the house. It was six of her seven felines. She hastily unbolted the door and let them in. Aside from something rust colored and dried to a tacky paste on Gemma's whiskers and neck, all the cats were unblemished. Only their paws were muddied and damp.

How the hell did they get out? When did they get out? Jillian wondered. *They were all here when we went to bed.*

She checked all the windows and doors again and froze when she looked out at the patio. It was covered with dozens of bloody paw prints. Without really thinking about what she was doing, Jillian pulled the garden hose over and rinsed down the patio. She cleaned each of the cats' paws, and then looked more closely at the substance on Gemma's fur. It looked like congealing blood. She wiped it away with a damp washcloth. She examined Gemma from head to toe and could find no cuts or wounds. Sleep would not come again for several long hours.

In the morning, Scott stayed home to get the kids off to school and let Jillian sleep in late. He knew what a terribly stressful day the previous one had been, with the visit from that crazy police detective who had shown up flinging accusations at her.

Once he left for work, Jillian showered and brewed a pot of coffee. She opened the newspaper to the front page and the coffee cup slipped from her hand. Jillian was only vaguely aware that the front of her robe was bathed in hot coffee and the shattered mug was scattered all over the floor.

The front page headline of the LA Times read:

VETERAN COLD CASE DETECTIVE FOUND MAULED TO DEATH

Below the headline were two photographs. The first, a car surrounded by crime scene tape. The picture was taken from a side view and showed the driver's side window smashed in. The only other thing visible in the photo was the side of the dead occupant's face. It was covered in vicious, criss-crossing slash marks. There was blood everywhere. The second photo was of a much younger Detective Keller Vaughn and was obviously taken from the police archives. He was clad in a crisp uniform and smiling his smug, cocky smile.

Jillian peered intently at that crime scene photo and a small smile played at her lips. "One would have thought what the detective lacked in good breeding he might have made up for in survival skills, but I guess not. Bad manners and couldn't even fend off a little kitty cat or two," she said as she folded up the newspaper.

As she swept up the broken shards from her coffee cup, Jillian began to laugh. Then she opened up a special treat for her beloved cats.

THE WIFE NEXT DOOR

WHEN THE LAST box was unpacked and the pizza had been delivered, Kate Frost popped the rings on two cans of beer and handed one to Frank. They toasted to Kate's new home. It was a four-year-old townhouse in a modest, well-kept neighborhood on the outskirts of Savannah.

Kate hoped the rumors of Southern hospitality would prove to be true in the days ahead. She was new in town and did not know a soul in Georgia.

It was a good sign when Frank returned from dropping off some cardboard moving cartons at the recycle bin and announced, "I just met your next door neighbor. Seems like a real nice fellow. The name is Tom."

Kate and Frank exchanged a smile and clicked their beer cans together once more. "To good neighbors," Kate said.

If anyone asked who the gentleman was that helped her move in, Kate would dust off the old story—Frank was her dad. Given the difference in their ages this was generally accepted without question. The truth was, they were not related. One could classify Frank as a close friend of the family. Kate referred to him as her wingman.

After seeing Frank off at the airport the following Monday, Kate was delighted to return home and find a plate of cookies on her doorstep with a note welcoming her to the neighborhood. It was signed Penny and Tom. Kate was pleased to see the gesture this soon after moving in. She didn't think she would make friends with her neighbors quite so quickly. In her experience these things usually took some time.

She was doubly pleased because the realization that their townhouses shared one common wall was not lost on her. When you live practically right on top of someone, it's always nice to be on friendly terms.

A few days later Kate knocked at the neighbor's door to return the dish the cookies had been delivered on.

Penny Langley was a pretty and petite brunette. She looked to be in her mid-thirties. She invited Kate in for a cup of coffee and the two women began a cautious friendship. The conversation lasted into the late afternoon and Penny invited Kate to come back for dinner. She gratefully accepted.

Tom Langley was a tall, muscular man with a fine mop of unruly black hair and a tidy goatee. His eyes were a pale and arresting blue that Kate found quite compelling.

Completing the family was Tom Junior, a mini-me of his father. TJ was nine years old and actively involved in softball league, martial arts classes and rock-climbing. He dominated most of the conversation at dinner, telling Kate about his many activities and school work. Kate adored him almost instantly.

She went home that night happy to have made her first friends in Savannah, Georgia. Since they would be living in such close proximity to one another it was a huge relief to discover she actually liked them, and the feeling was obviously mutual.

It was a friendship Kate would cultivate carefully, and it would continue to grow stronger over the next year.

Within thirteen months the couple and Kate were nearly inseparable and seemed more like family than neighbors. They ate dinner together nearly every night and had long since exchanged house keys. They took down the small fence separating their back patios and turned the area into one common backyard. In the summer they all vacationed together in Cabo.

Kate was never very forthcoming about her past and what brought her to Savannah from California in the first place, but she did offer enough information to keep Penny and Tom from trying to pry any deeper. The sketchy and tragic story included a new husband who had fallen from a high scaffolding on a construction site at a painfully young age. There was also mention of a miscarriage and enough life insurance to start life over in Georgia after her husband's untimely death.

Kate was twenty-six years old, which was just too young to be a widow. Learning of her past, Penny and Tom grew very protective over her and watched cautiously out the window every time a young suitor arrived to pick her up for a date. They wanted to stand guard at the edge of Kate's life and make sure no one caused her any pain ever again. She seemed so fragile and vulnerable. She still could not speak of her lost husband without tears filling her hazel eyes.

The similarities between Penny and Kate were eerie. They liked the same foods, the same activities, and sometimes even finished one another's sentences. While Kate was taller than Penny and had blond hair instead of brunette, they wore their hair in the same style. Other parallels were unmistakable, too. They were both possessed of the same petite build and favored the same colors and styles of clothing. The two women often borrowed each other's wardrobe. At times neither could even remember what article belonged to which woman. They had become just like sisters.

Kate began working a string of unsatisfying office jobs and never stayed at one for very long. The first job she found that she actually enjoyed was as a front-desk clerk at a hotel. It ended abruptly one evening when she came home pale and shaking. She tearfully informed Penny and Tom that she had been held up at gunpoint by a man wearing a ski mask.

They were horrified, and insisted she leave such a dangerous place at once. Tom worked in sales for a successful software manufacturer. After the crime at the hotel, Tom spoke to his boss about bringing Kate on at his office part-time. While the company didn't really have any job openings, Tom was one of their top salesmen and they wanted to keep him happy, so they created a position for Kate. It was easy and fun work that paid more than it should have. It also came with a full cache of benefits. Kate and Tom ate lunch together the three days a week Kate was in the office.

For the first six months everything was fine and the job went well. Kate was happy and the company was pleased with her work. The situation seemed ideal, until one day when everything changed.

It happened on a Wednesday, while Tom looked across the table at lunch and discovered his feelings for Kate had shifted dramatically. It had happened so suddenly and so quietly that it blindsided him. He was a happily married man, but he was falling in love with his next door neighbor. Having always been honest with his wife, and never spending one unfaithful day apart, he was horrified to discover he could not turn the unwanted feelings off. The force of his attraction to Kate scared him. The more he was around her the stronger the desire was growing. The only saving grace was that neither his wife nor Kate seemed aware of his ardor. Tom prayed he could keep them both oblivious long enough to figure out how to make his feelings for her go away.

After struggling for three weeks with his emotions, he lost the battle. Every time he caught the scent of Kate's perfume or felt her nearness when she brushed against him, he would become instantly and uncomfortably aroused. He could not go on this way.

It was with a tremendously guilty heart that he decided to confide in his wife about his new-found feelings for their neighbor. It was only a matter of time, before, unable to control himself, a line would be crossed from which there could be no turning back. Tom's obsession had reached the point where Kate occupied not only his every waking thought, but she followed him into his dreams as well.

The last thing he wanted was to start up some tawdry, back-street affair with the woman who lived next door and spent nearly every day with his family. He couldn't do that to Penny, and he couldn't do it to Kate either.

She had become almost like a second mother to Tom Junior. She chauffeured him to his many after-school activities on days when Penny was busy, and often kept the boy at her house when Tom travelled for business and Penny accompanied him. Kate had nursed both the boy and his parents through flus, food poisoning and colds. He and Penny had flown to California with Kate and helped her clean out her father's belongings after his passing the previous fall. They never left her side during the long weeks of grieving. Tom even spent several nights sleeping on her sofa when she could not bear to be alone in the stillness of the night.

Tom did not anticipate his wife taking this declaration of his feelings well. In fourteen years of marriage, this was one conversation neither of them ever saw coming. They were always a team, always together. While many of their friends had affairs, or divorced for any number of reasons, they were always the couple everyone envied. And there was no difference between the way the world perceived them and what happened behind closed doors. They truly were a happily married couple.

Tom worried not only about the blow his marriage would sustain, but how it would affect Penny's friendship with Kate. The two women were closer than sisters.

After putting their son to bed and settling on the couch for a glass of wine before retiring, Tom took his wife's hand. "I need to talk to you," he said, his voice betraying his nervousness.

Concerned, Penny put her glass down and turned to her husband. "What's wrong? You look like you're about to cry."

"I have to tell you something and I am afraid you are going to hate me." At this point the tears did come. He dissolved weeping and covered his face with his hands.

Penny grasped her husband's shoulders and waited for the sobs to diminish. "You are scaring the hell out of me, Tommy, so you better just tell me what's going on. Are we bankrupt or something?"

"I think I have fallen in love with Kate," he sputtered.

There wasn't the hurt and shocked gasp of surprise he anticipated. Penny didn't throw the wine in his face. In fact, she didn't even look all that surprised.

She offered one deep sigh. Wrinkling her nose like she just smelled something foul, she asked, "Does Kate know? You haven't... you know... done anything, have you?"

He vehemently shook his head. "Oh, Jesus, Penny, no! Of course not."

"Well, that's something anyway."

They were quiet for a long time before Penny spoke again. "I suppose we should have seen this coming. I mean, I am pretty much in love with her, too. It's like we are married to her, too, without the... well you know."

Tom's eyes flew open in shock. "You mean you want to... uh, you're attracted to her, too?" he gasped.

The look of disgust his wife shot him caused his cheeks to grow red.

Penny replied, "Ewww, no, you idiot. Get your head out of the Penthouse Forum, would you. That's not what I meant."

"Sorry," he mumbled.

"What I meant was, it's like she's part of our family. And I want to keep it that way. You better make damn sure you watch how you behave around her. Don't do anything you're going to regret, or you will lose both of us, champ. I mean it."

"I don't want to do anything, Penny. I love you! I want to stay married to you. I just don't know what to do about these feelings. I never wanted to even tell you, but I had too. I don't know how to fix this, and I can't go on this way. It's.... well, it's very difficult to be around her, to even sit next to her." Tom held up his hand as though his wife had objected. "I'm sorry, I know you don't want to hear this. It has to be killing you."

Penny rolled her eyes. "Don't flatter yourself," she said dryly. "I don't much like it, but it's not exactly killing me either. You haven't touched her, thank God." She looked to her husband again with one eyebrow raised.

Tom saw the unspoken question in her gaze and shook his head violently. "I swear to you, I haven't. She has no idea how I'm feeling."

Penny nodded, satisfied. "Good. Keep it that way. Look, I am not going to get mad at you just because you have feelings for her. I suppose you can't help that. As long as you don't act on them."

"I wouldn't do that to you," Tom said sincerely.

Penny frowned. "Even if you did, honestly, I can't see her flying into bed with you. Despite how desirable you seem to think you are, Kate likes things just the way they are. She wouldn't be jumping for joy if you sprung this on her, Romeo. In case you've forgotten, she isn't sitting at home pining away for you. She's out with a different guy every weekend."

Tom had to laugh. He could always count on Penny to set him straight and put his feet back on the ground. She had always been his voice of reason in any crisis. Even now, when he was confessing his desire to cheat on her with the woman next door, she was still acting practically and sensibly. He sure hoped it would stay that way in the days ahead. Three months down the road he would prefer they weren't the subject of a love-triangle-gone-wrong episode on *Dateline*, with one of them lying dead. Most likely him.

"We just have to figure out how to deal with this mess," Penny said.

"So, you aren't mad at me?"

"I'm not thrilled with you, but, no, I'm not really mad. It was only a matter of time before something like this happened. She comes with us on vacation, for God's sake. Our relationship with her really is just like having another person in the marriage."

"I'm sorry, Penny. I never meant for this to happen," Tom muttered.

"Well, at least you were honest with me." Rising from the couch, she said, "I'm going to bed. I don't want to talk about this anymore tonight. I need to think."

With that, she turned off the light, leaving Tom sitting alone in the darkness. He couldn't say he felt great, but he had to admit that he was very relieved to finally have the confession out in the open. He drained his wine glass and followed his wife upstairs.

The next day Penny had come up with a solution to Tom's dilemma. While he assumed his wife would be the one totally astounded when he told her of his feelings for Kate, it was he who nearly fell out of his chair when he heard Penny's proposed resolution.

All the color drained from his face and he stared open-mouthed at his wife. "You want to do what?" he asked, sure he must have misunderstood.

"Look, Tom, I'm just being practical here. If I thought this was just some itch you needed to scratch, I would probably tell you to go ahead and see if she'll have you for a night. But I can see it's more than that. This isn't just a phase you are going through—some mid-life crisis thing that will blow over in the springtime. Kate is a part of us. This is really the only solution that makes any sense. There is no reset button on feelings and they don't just disappear, no matter how much we might want them to."

"And you would be okay with…"

"Okay? Hell no! But, I think I can learn to live with it. The alternative is we lose her—and then we lose us because you blame me and I blame you. It really is the only way."

While it wasn't unusual for Kate to eat dinner at the Langleys' table, it was out of the ordinary for Tom Junior not to join them, and for Penny to break out the good dishes and grill Filet Mignon. It wasn't any of their birthdays and no one was celebrating anything, so she did wonder just what was going on.

After dessert was served they told her. Like Penny, Kate wasn't really all that surprised to learn of Tom's attraction to her. Perhaps women are more savvy about these things than men are, or maybe she just wasn't blind to Tom's too-long glances, or the uncomfortable shift he always had to give his trousers every time she was close to him.

Kate listened with calm thoughtfulness as Penny laid out their proposal. With wry amusement she wondered just what Frank would think of this.

Both Penny and Tom took it as a good sign when their neighbor did not spring from the table and flee from their house quick enough to leave skid marks in her wake.

After a silence that felt like it had lasted an eternity, Kate finally spoke. "Polygamy is not legal. You both know that, right?"

Penny rapidly bobbed her head up and down. "Of course. It wouldn't be a legal marriage naturally, but it would be a commitment of our hearts. We will have a ceremony, take our vows, buy you a ring, and then we will all be married. All three of us. We love you, Kate. With all our hearts."

Kate looked back and forth between them, not masking her distaste. "And then what? I don't play for both teams. In all this time nothing ever got weird. There was never any talk of ménage à trois, or anything kinky between us—and just so you know, I am not into anything like that. I didn't think you guys were either. You are like the best couple I know!"

Penny looked only slightly embarrassed as she soldiered on. Man, was Tom ever going to owe her if they got through this conversation with their relationship with Kate still afloat. He was sitting there mute like a mannequin and forcing her to do all the heavy lifting. She wished he would say something to help quell the horrified look from Kate's face.

"Okay, Kate. I am going to stop trying to sugar coat this and just tell you the truth. Tom went and fell in love with you."

Tom groaned audibly.

"Whoa!" Kate shot up from the table and started for the door.

Penny cried, "Hang on! Please, sit down and let me explain." She looked to Tom, who continued to stare miserably at his shoes. He was too humiliated to speak or even make eye contact with either woman. She wasn't going to get any help from that direction.

Penny hurried on, "He still loves me and wants to stay married, but he fell for you, too. It just happened, it's no one's fault."

Kate plopped back down in her chair. She sighed and said, "Things like this don't just happen."

Penny shrugged. "People are human. Life gets messy sometimes."

"I know, but I didn't think it got this messy—at least not between us."

Penny was relieved to see Kate sit down and stop inching her way toward the exit. "Look, Kate, I don't know how you feel about Tom personally, but I know you are happy with our current arrangement and that you love Tom Junior like your own. None of us want to lose you."

When Kate said nothing, Penny asked, "Do you want to leave us now? Do you want to stop being a part of our family anymore because of this? If you do, then just say the word. We'll give you back your house key, we'll put the partition back on the patio and we'll let you go. It would kill me to do that, and it would break my son's heart, but we would do it if that's what you want."

In a tiny voice Tom mumbled, "Would kill me, too."

Kate looked back and forth between the couple for a long moment. Finally she expelled a long shuddering breath. "Jeez, of course I don't want to lose you guys. Either of you! And I especially don't want to lose TJ. This just really took me by surprise. It's totally crazy."

Penny shrugged. "Is it? There are all kinds of families. This might not be the traditional norm, but we aren't the first people to think of it, you know. There are whole colonies of polygamists out there. They even have reality shows on TV about them."

Kate nodded. "That's true, I guess. Besides, I have about forty-six of your blouses in my closet, Pen, so breaking up is out of the question."

They all chuckled nervously at the joke, and a little of the tension crept from the room.

"Exactly how would this work?" Kate asked.

"Not that much would change. I don't want Tom to have an affair with you. I want to be a part of your relationship, just like you are a part of ours. That's why the ceremony and the rings. We want you to marry both of us."

When Penny saw the look on Kate's face, she hastily added, "Marry both of us, but only sleep with Tom. Because, as I am sure you know, I don't play for both teams either." Kate exhaled a noisy breath. "Well that's a relief. Okay, go on." *Oh boy, Frank is gonna love this*, she thought.

Glad that Kate was still willing to listen, Penny laid out the rest of their plan. "You would still live in your house and we would live in ours. Tom would spend half the nights here, and half with you—I mean, if that's what you would want. I suppose we should ask...do you have...do you have any um, romantic...or sexual feelings for him? Or is this just too creepy?"

Now it was Kate's turn to look away embarrassed. She shrugged. "The truth is I have always been attracted to you, Tom," Kate said, pulling him back into the conversation. "I just never would have acted on those feelings because of how much I love Penny."

Tom reached across the table and took her hand. "So, you would consider an arrangement like this?"

Kate squeezed his hand once and then released it. "Maybe. I don't know. I sure in hell haven't found Mr. Right anywhere else. Let me think about everything. It's a lot to absorb."

Tom hastily added, "I don't want things to be weird between us now, whatever you decide."

"Too late," both women responded at the same time.

Six years later

Kate, Penny and Tom celebrated their sixth wedding anniversary at a fine Italian Bistro. The mood was somewhat subdued, and Kate was anxious to return home. While Tom Junior was a responsible teenager, she didn't like leaving him alone for too long with Chloe. The daughter Kate had given Tom two years after they were married could be a handful. The baby was a happy accident that the whole family loved dearly. She had just turned four and would be starting pre-school in the fall.

In the beginning, right after Kate had married the Langleys', the adjustment period had been much harder for Penny than anticipated. She'd cried herself to sleep many nights, while envisioning what was going on in the house next door with sickening clarity.

She dealt with her jealousies quietly and eventually came to accept the new arrangement. Though, not a day passed when she didn't regret suggesting this insane solution to Tom's wanderlust in the first place. Up until Kate's pregnancy she hadn't fully realized the situation she had put them all in. What had she been thinking?

Kate's transition from friend to wife was much easier. She knew Penny and Tom as a married couple from the moment she met them, so imagining them together sexually didn't bother her at all. Not even after she and Tom became intimate.

Initially, when the couple approached her with their strange proposal, she thought it was a terrible idea. She had called Frank in California and discussed the situation at great length with him, repeatedly arguing this was not the way the plan was supposed to go. Frank was adamant the arrangement could work. Because Kate trusted his judgment on most matters, she had reluctantly agreed to the faux marriage.

For Tom, his feelings for Kate had only intensified over the years. He was not only hopelessly in love with her, he was completely bewitched and under her spell. He would never admit this to Penny, but his feelings for her had faded since Kate joined their family. It was to Kate that his heart completely belonged.

Since the birth of Chloe, he had given a great deal of thought to divorcing his first wife. All he wanted was to be legally married to Kate. He had grown to hate the entire set-up. He wanted to spend every night with Kate. He hated being away from her for even a single evening, let alone three or four nights a week.

Penny was no fool. She knew her husband's kiss had grown cold. Since the birth of Chloe, his gaze was always settled lovingly on Kate and the baby. Sometimes Penny thought Tom forgot she was even in the room.

Fortunately their son was busy with all the demands of high school and extracurricular activities, so he failed to see the chasm that had widened between his parents over the last few years. As far as the boy was concerned, not much changed after Kate joined their family. He was too young at the time to fully understand the implications of his father taking a second wife. Since Kate had been like a second mother to him anyway, the structure of his family seemed status quo.

On the eve of their sixth and final anniversary dinner, things weighed heavily on Kate's mind. After six years, being the second wife had taken quite a toll.

One of the main problems confronting Kate was financial. The money from her first husband's life insurance policy was finally running dry. While her arrangement with the Langleys' took care of most of her daughter's needs, Kate was still largely financially responsible for all of her own expenses. The part-time job with Tom's company was not going to be enough anymore. As the money from the life insurance had dwindled, Kate realized everything was starting to catch up with her and she knew things were going to have to change.

When she first married the couple, this was not how she envisioned things turning out. She never dreamed she would remain a part of this unholy trio for such a long time.

The fault lay with her daughter. Chloe had not been part of her plan. The pregnancy had been an accident—one Frank badgered her relentlessly to terminate before Tom and Penny could find out.

Kate refused. She loved her daughter with all her heart from the moment she found out she was carrying her. The abortion battle was one of the few Frank ever lost.

The last four years coasted by in a blur. Kate had been totally focused on Chloe, and nothing else. All Frank's protests about how Kate should be moving their agenda forward became nothing more than static in the background.

With the money running out she was finally forced to listen to him. Chloe was just getting ready to start school and Kate needed to be there to drop her off in the morning and pick her up in the afternoon. Working full-time was out of the question.

While she knew Penny would perform whatever motherly duties were needed in the interest of keeping Tom happy, Chloe was a very painful reminder that her husband was in love with another woman.

Kate knew Penny's bed was half empty, even on the nights Tom shared it with her. Though his body might be lying beside his wife, his heart was still very much with the woman next door. Kate would not allow her child to be on the receiving end of Penny's resentment. If she was locked up in an office working, she would be unable to protect her.

Like Penny, Kate wished they had never entered into the unconventional arrangement. This was one time when Frank's sage wisdom had proven faulty. Nothing had worked out the way she thought it would. It was time to pull the plug.

At the conclusion of that very sad anniversary dinner, when Penny went home to her lonely bed, Kate sat Tom down and told him things needed to change. She could no longer play house with a married couple. She told him, "As of this moment, we are officially divorced. Since it was never legal anyway, we won't need any messy paperwork."

Tom was devastated. He cried and pleaded with Kate to change her mind. He swore he would divorce Penny and marry her. He promised to give Kate all the money she needed to stay home with Chloe. She would never have to work at all. He was desperate and would have sold his soul to the devil to keep her.

Kate's resolve remained firm. She sent Tom home to Penny, vowing never to allow him into her bed again. He cried himself to sleep on the couch, with his hands pressed firmly against the wall that separated him from his beloved.

The next day his hostility assaulted Penny like a freezing winter wind. While he said little, he could not keep the loathing for his first wife from his eyes. He blamed her for Kate's decision to leave, even though Penny was completely unaware of it. She did not learn until later that day what Kate had done.

When Tom went to work, Kate told Penny of her decision. She saw the momentary and nearly blinding relief flood her friend's eyes, and knew she had made the right decision. She was the interloper here. She always had been, even though the doomed arrangement had been Penny's idea in the first place. Penny hugged Kate with panicky tightness and sobbed, "Thank you," against her neck.

Kate could feel Penny's desperate tears on her skin. She held her for only a brief moment before returning to her own home.

She had a lot to think about. How was she going to break it to Tom that she planned to sell the townhouse and leave Savannah?

She wasn't sure who was going to take the news worse: Tom or Frank. Neither man was going to like it, but she knew there was no other choice—no matter what Frank would have to say about it. Frank needed to accept that sometimes plans changed. She could no longer carry out the scheme that landed her in Savannah in the first place. Things had grown far too complicated.

In the weeks that followed, both men convinced her not to leave the state. Frank insisted their plans could still be salvaged, and Tom gave in to her every demand.

When Chloe started pre-school he began providing much greater financial support. He bit his tongue, voicing not a single complaint, even though his own household was now coming up short for the bills every month. He would do anything to keep Kate next door.

His relationship with Penny fractured even further. It felt more like a thorn lodged in his side than a marriage. In his heart, he still blamed her for Kate leaving him.

Penny was completely bewildered by her husband's animosity toward her. He went out of his way to pick quarrels with her daily. She did everything she could to try to please him, but his bitterness only grew with each passing week.

Tom felt completely trapped. With so much money going to Kate, a divorce would bankrupt him. He suffered in silence, long-ing for Kate's touch and praying she would change her mind and take him back.

Within just a few months the impossible financial strain of maintaining both households became too much to juggle. The en-tire house of cards was on the verge of collapse. Adding to Tom's misery, he was no closer to winning Kate back despite the horrible position he had put himself in financially for her. Life without her was worse than a death sentence. He was at the end of his rope.

When Tom was sure he was going to choke to death on his sorrow, he made the only decision he thought available to him to win Kate back. He could see no other choice than to kill Penny.

Tom asked Penny to accompany him on a business trip. It had been a long time since she had travelled with him on one of these sojourns. Over the last few years it was always Kate who went, leaving Penny home to care for the children. Penny was delighted and thought this meant he was taking the first step in healing the distance between them.

Tom visited Kate the night before the trip. He told her, "I know you don't want to hurt Penny and that's why you have convinced yourself we can't be together anymore. I promise you, after this weekend, Penny won't be hurting any longer. You have to trust me."

"Tom, what are you talking about? Penny will always be hurt by what happened between us. Don't kid yourself. There is nothing you can do to change that except be the kind of husband she deserves now."

Tom nodded decisively. His eyes darted around madly. "I can fix this. You just have to trust me. Everything will be different come Monday, and you and I will be able to be together again. Nothing will stand in our way."

When Kate lay down in her bed that night, sleep remained elusive. She knew Tom very well, and all his cryptic words could mean only one thing.

Just like six years before, when Penny and Tom approached her with their strange proposal, she wasn't terribly surprised to realize Tom was now planning to murder his wife. No, she really wasn't surprised at all. Kate, of course, would have no choice but to go to the authorities.

After dropping Chloe at school, Kate made the drive to the police department. When she asked to speak to a detective and explained the nature of her visit, the secretary gave her a hard look. "You have information about a murder, you say?" she asked incredulously.

Kate nodded. "I don't think it's happened yet, but it's going to. I hope someone can stop it."

The secretary led her to an interview room and told her a detective would be with her shortly. She offered Kate coffee, which she declined.

Ten minutes later, a short, marginally overweight detective entered the room and sat down. After introducing himself as Detective Burke, he asked, "So, what's this about a murder?"

Kate took a deep breath and began explaining her unconventional, ersatz marriage to Tom and Penny. The detective listened for a few minutes, and then interrupted. "Let me get this straight. Your husband is married to another woman? He's a bigamist? And you knew about this other wife when you married him?"

Kate sighed. "It isn't exactly like that. I was married to both of them. It's hard to explain." She didn't like what she saw in this detective's eyes. He was looking at her the way people looked at the bearded lady at a carnival. And worse, like he didn't believe a word she was saying.

"And you think your husband is going to try and kill his first wife so he can be with you? Is that right?" The detective raised his fingers in air-quotes on the word husband. This wasn't going well at all.

Kate nodded uncertainly.

Detective Burke rose. "Will you excuse me a moment?"

Once he left the room, Kate became very nervous. The detective was gone for what felt like an eternity, but was only about twenty minutes. She toyed with the idea of calling Frank from her cell phone, but what could he do? And besides, who knew if they had recorders or cameras hidden in the walls.

When Burke returned he had another man with him. The newcomer introduced himself as Sergeant Randal Sherman. He told Kate to call him Randy. She liked him much more than the first detective instantly.

"Ms. Frost, Charlie here tells me you are afraid that a man you were involved with is planning on murdering his wife. I hate to make you go over this again, but would you mind explaining your relationship with the couple to me, and why it is you think a crime is going to take place."

Kate took a deep breath and once more told the story. She liked what she saw in Sherman's eyes a whole lot more than she had in Burke's. It was sympathy she saw there. And something else dancing right behind his kindness; a look Kate had been seeing in men's eyes since she hit puberty. That was good. She knew the look well and even had a name for it. She called it the "Savior Stare." The last time she'd seen it reflected back at her was in Tom's arresting blue eyes all those years ago, when she'd told him and Penny the story of being held up by a masked gunman at the hotel where she was working.

She had fabricated that story. The truth was, she just didn't want to work there anymore. The job was doing nothing to advance the goals she and Frank were pursuing when she moved to Georgia. Things were stalled and they needed a kick-start.

Some men just can't resist being the hero. Especially when a pretty girl—the proverbial damsel in distress, is involved. Kate wasn't sure if it was a subconscious thing or not, but these men all believed if they could ride in on their trusty white charger and rescue the fair maiden, the next sound they heard would be silk sliding against skin as the grateful maiden slid her panties to the floor and opened her legs in gratitude. She'd seen it, and if she was to be honest, used it to her advantage, on a number of occasions over the years. It was how she landed her first husband, not to mention the cushy job in Tom's office that ultimately led to his undoing.

Kate was grateful to see The Savior Stare on Detective Sherman's face now. Things just became a great deal easier.

Detective Burke faded into the background as Randy Sherman sprang into action. Once he obtained the information of where Tom and Penny were traveling, he alerted authorities there to converge on the hotel in case the couple arrived early. He notified the state Highway Patrol and put out a BOLO for the Langleys' car.

He commended Kate for coming forward and trying to prevent a possible tragedy. When he patted her hand, and his own lingered just a beat too long, Kate knew she'd found quite a bit more than just a diligent officer of the law.

Unfortunately, it was all just a little too late to save Penny. The Highway Patrol spotted Tom's car on a wide desolate patch of interstate. He was caught with Penny's lifeless body in his arms. The police had rolled in behind him just as he was trying to dispose of her remains down a ravine. He was taken into custody without incident.

After Kate had given birth to Chloe, she and the Langleys' changed their life insurance policies. If anything happened to any one of the trio, the money would be split evenly between the surviving spouses. Because Tom was charged with her murder, he would not be eligible to receive one dime of the money from Penny's policy. It all went to Kate.

Tom tried to phone her repeatedly from jail to ask her to hire an attorney for him, but she would not take his calls.

Sergeant Randal Sherman was a great comfort to Kate during the difficult months that followed. He spent nearly every evening at her house and helped her tend to Chloe. Within just a few months of Penny's murder he moved in to Kate's townhouse. They were married nearly six months before Tom Langley stood trial for the murder of his wife.

In an odd coincidence, on the fourth day of the trial, it was Sergeant Sherman who was assigned to transport Tom Langley to the courthouse.

The accident was unheard of in the history of police transport vehicles. What should have been a routine three mile drive from the holding facility to the courthouse, ended with the unmarked police vehicle wrapped around a telephone pole. Both the driver and the single occupant were killed. After an exhaustive investigation, no cause for the crash was ever determined. It was ruled a most unfortunate accident.

Southern California
Five Months Later

Kate sat on the couch inside Frank's dismal apartment in the San Fernando Valley nursing a glass of red wine and listening to the rain patter against the windows. Chloe occupied herself with cartoons jumping mindlessly across the television in the bedroom.

Kate said, "So, are you retiring since the last one paid out the trifecta? Maybe now you can pursue that acting thing full-time."

Frank chuckled. "Nah. I'm still an unemployed actor, but the work with you is steady. I think I will stay on if you don't mind."

"You sure?" she asked dryly. "I notice you don't much like waiting when the payday gets delayed. And of course, you do realize, this last one was a fluke? Like hitting the lottery."

"Are you complaining?" Frank raised an eyebrow.

"Not about the money, but I don't want you thinking something like this could ever happen again. I really didn't want anything to happen to Penny."

"I know. You made it very clear after Chloe was born that no harm was to come to your wife," Frank chuckled. "And I certainly wasn't going to take Tommy boy out while Penny stood to get half the money from his policy."

"Well, you know we couldn't have taken them both out. I told you the polygamy thing was a bad idea, Frank. I would have been the prime suspect. They would have dove into my past and found out my last husband had met up with a rather early demise, too. That wasn't a chance we could take."

Frank shrugged. "Fortunately Tom solved that problem for us. Imagine getting caught with his dead wife in his arms by the side of a highway."

"Frank, do not procure anymore married ones. It doesn't work out well. TJ was collateral damage I really wish could have been avoided. Poor kid got shipped off to an aunt in Delaware."

"You know, honey, there isn't exactly a huge surplus of straight, single men out there walking around with million dollar life insurance policies on themselves. They are hard to find. And frankly, the baby was why everything went south. You got soft. It wasn't really the polygamy thing that derailed the train."

"What do you mean?"

Frank hooked a thumb toward the bedroom. "No one told you to get pregnant. You took your eye off the end-game and wasted time playing Mommy, instead of getting the job done."

Kate shot Frank an ill-tempered look. "That's my child you're talking about. And I don't know what you're complaining about. Didn't I fly out and help you pack up all your things when you got evicted from that place on Laurel Canyon."

"As I recall, it was Tom and Penny who did all the work. You told them they were packing up the home of your deceased father— who, by the way, I had lunch with yesterday. He sends his love."

"The point is, I have always been there for you. Despite how long this particular payday took, I still had your back."

"I know, Kate. But you were just supposed to follow the script. Get Tom Langley to leave his wife, marry you, and then change the beneficiary on his life insurance policy to his lovely new bride. You weren't supposed to start having babies and pretend to be a suburban soccer mom. The whole thing—including Tom Langley's untimely demise, should have taken a year and a half max. Letting them totally jack up the insurance so badly after the kid was born wasn't in the script either."

Exasperated, Kate replied, "Well, I don't write the scripts. This one wrote itself. Tom was a tough one to reel in. He really wasn't the cheating kind."

Frank laughed. "No, not the cheating kind. Just the murdering kind when he didn't get his own way. Such a prince."

"Good point. But let's not speak ill of the dead."

Frank looked at Kate speculatively. "In the end you didn't seem like you even wanted to cash that bastard in. Why is that?"

Kate shifted uncomfortably. "Because he was the father of my kid, Frank. You never understood how that changed things."

"When did you get so fucking sentimental? His sperm contribution shouldn't have changed anything—least of all after he killed Penny."

"By then it wasn't up to me. I really didn't think Tom could meet with any unfortunate accidents while he was in police custody. Look, we got three for the price of one, so what are we arguing about?"

"Yes, my little femme fatale, we did get three. How did you get Randy to make you the beneficiary on his policy right after you two were married?"

Kate shrugged. "I didn't. Believe it or not, that was his idea. Poor Randy. I never wanted anything to happen to him either. That was really a shame."

Frank grinned. He looked a little like a shark. "Yeah, poor Randy. Freaky accident, huh? Both husband number two and husband number three with one stone. Or should I say one telephone pole?"

Kate glared at Frank. "I've been meaning to ask, exactly how much did you have to do with that accident?"

Frank remained silent, but the satisfied smirk on his face told Kate all she needed to know. Sometimes her partner in crime really scared her.

Kate shook off the shiver that racked her shoulders and dismissed the conversation. "I don't know how many more times we can do this before people start calling me the black widow. The body count is reaching the point where someone is going to connect the dots."

Frank nodded. "I've been thinking about that. Besides, the doe-eyed, damsel in distress routine doesn't work so well at your age anymore. Sorry dear, but you are getting a little too old to be as effective as you once were. The next mark should probably be our last."

"Gee, thanks. What next mark? You found someone already?"

In his best game-show host voice, Frank boomed, "Pack your bags, little lady, and get ready for an all-expense paid vacation to Vermont."

Kate wrinkled her nose. "Really? You couldn't have found someplace warmer?"

"You'll like this one. He's a doctor. Donates all his money to charity."

"Is he cute?"

Frank handed her a photograph.

Kate scanned it and remarked, "Not as cute as Tom, but I can live with anyone for a year, I suppose."

"A whole year? You should be ordering the headstone in half that time. This one won't take long," Frank commented.

Kate rolled her eyes. "Yeah, that's what you said about the last one."

LILITH'S WAY

THE JULY 15TH meeting of the Rattlesnake UFO Club was a sweltering affair. The air conditioning at the church was on the fritz again. But the members were a dedicated bunch, and life in the Arizona desert was never all that cool anyway. What was a little sweat among friends?

While the Reverend Carter Littlejohn didn't much care for renting out the basement of First Baptist to the UFO group (referred to in the privacy of his mind as *the Wackadoodle Breeding Ground*), a fifty-dollar rental fee was a fifty-dollar rental fee. As long as they weren't sacrificing babies or kittens down there, and they rinsed out the coffee pot at the end of the evening, then what was the harm?

With the air conditioning malfunctioning more often than not, the only other groups who were still willing to rent the basement meeting room were the anonymous folks: alcoholics, druggies, and the like. Besides, the reverend enjoyed seeing Lilith Chalmers when she came to pay the rental fee and set up for the meeting. While the Daisy Duke shorts she typically wore were not appropriate attire for a church in the reverend's opinion, his eyes still followed the exaggerated sway of her hips as she descended the stairs to the basement. On this night, he noticed that both of Lilith's hands were wrapped in bandages. He wondered what had happened, but didn't ask. Given her eccentricities, he wasn't sure he really wanted to know.

Lilith was a good looking lady—in that *prettiest girl in the trailer park* kind of way. She came by her blond hair and ample bosom naturally. There were no bottles of Miss Clairol buried in the trash out back. Lilith was well aware of the effect she had on men. She had learned at a young age how to work those looks to her advantage. Since her divorce, her breasts alone had paid for many a night of drinking and shooting pool down at the Leopard Spot Tavern on Route 179. She subscribed to the belief, and history had proven; cleavage was a girl's best friend.

Scores of men had spent the last penny of their paychecks on those drinks, in hopes of seeing Lilith's breasts in a much more up-close-and-personal way. They were always disappointed at the end of the evening. Lilith didn't sell her charms for the price of a few gin and tonics.

Men rarely turned her head. If you wanted to woo Lilith, the secret wasn't in plying her full of booze. (She could drink most men under the table.) And it wasn't in complimenting her on her good looks either. The secret was in telling her about the time you saw a UFO hurtling through the midnight sky. Or better yet, the genuine alien encounter you had with the extraterrestrials manning the craft to which you bore witness.

Lilith lived for the day when the mother ship would call her home. Most people write off characters with such vivid imaginations (the Wackadoodle Breeding Ground) as crazy folks. But, if you knew Lilith's story, it wouldn't seem quite so strange.

You see, apart from a pretty face and high breasts, Lilith had other gifts. Ones she discovered at a very young age. These particular talents came in handy when your mother was a drunk and your father was...well...who knew? When you had two younger brothers in need of food and care, and you were only a child yourself, you grew up pretty quick.

When she was just eight years old, Lilith realized she wasn't like other children. Home alone with her younger siblings, she had just put them to bed and done the dinner dishes. Her mother had thoughtfully not left for the Leopard Spot until the children were fed this evening.

Lilith sat down to do her homework. Her neighbor, an ill-tempered old man with bad teeth, had been yelling at Dozer to quit barking for the last hour or so. There was a party across the street, and the noise made their dog anxious. He was very protective of all the Chalmers children, but was particularly fond of Lilith. She always made sure he had food, fresh water, and warm blankets to sleep on.

When your mother was away at the bars most nights, it was of great comfort to have Dozer standing sentry between you and the rest of the world once darkness fell. Lilith found the dog's barking a reassuring sound against the night. To her ears, it sounded like a warning to any ill-meaning foe intent on causing her or her brothers harm. They wouldn't get past Dozer without a fight. A fight they would likely lose!

To the neighbor, however, the dog's barking was a nuisance. He yelled at the German Shepard a few times. When that didn't work, he hurled a full bottle of beer into the yard aiming for Dozer's head. Fortunately, he missed his target. But, the bottle shattered against the back door of the house, scaring Lilith and her brothers half to death.

She cautiously opened the door just wide enough to allow the dog entry into the kitchen. As she was closing it, a slipper-shod foot kicked its way in. Lilith stumbled backward and nearly fell as the owner of that foot barged into the kitchen. Spraying spittle, he demanded to speak to Lilith's mother.

Terrified, and not wanting to admit there was no adult in the house, Lilith stammered some vague reply about her mother being asleep in the back room.

When the neighbor pushed past her and started down the hallway toward the rear of the house, Lilith's terror gave way to sheer rage. "You can't go back there," she cried, angrily.

The intruder made no move to retreat. Instead, he shoved her youngest brother, Seth, aside when he valiantly tried to block his path. Lilith ran up behind the man and grabbed onto his coat, meaning to pull him back. When her hands connected with the fabric, what looked like a million, tiny luminescent sparks burst from her fingertips in a blinding flash. The narrow walls of the hallway were instantly ablaze with brilliant light. The preternatural radiance temporarily transformed little Seth into a shimmering angel before her.

As Lilith was struggling to comprehend what had just happened, the man began to jerk crazily. He turned into a marionette on wildly juddering strings, run by an evil puppet master. All at once he slumped to the floor in a dead heap.

Lilith was vaguely aware of her four-year-old brother beside her. Staring wide-eyed, he gasped, "Oh man! Lily, that was bitchin'." (He'd recently picked up the word somewhere, and for the last week everything was "bitchin" to young Seth.)

Lilith splayed her fingers. She stood looking at her hands in disbelief. They tingled and she felt a numbing warmness spreading through her fingertips. She peered dumbstruck at the lifeless body lying by her feet, and then looked back at her slowly cooling fingers. "Uh oh," she sighed, "This isn't good."

By now, both of her younger siblings flanked her on either side. "Better call Uncle Frank," Josh advised sagely, poking a toe into the prone body on the floor. "I think he's toast."

Josh was only six, but he was right. There was no one else to call but their mom's brother. The old man, did indeed, appear to be toast. Lilith would worry about the freaky light show her fingers had put on later.

When situations beyond her ability to handle arose, Lilith turned to Uncle Frank. In other words: Those things which required the help of a responsible adult. Of course, usually the calls were nothing more urgent than needing a bag of dog food, or enough money for a school book. This predicament was new.

Reluctantly, Lilith went to the phone and dialed her uncle's cell phone number. A sleepy woman's voice answered the phone. When Lilith identified herself, she mumbled something and passed the phone to Frank Chalmers.

Once Lilith explained the situation as best she could, her uncle didn't seem terribly surprised by what had occurred. He asked her the oddest question, "Do you know if he has a pacemaker?"

Lilith didn't even know what a pacemaker was. However, on the night she discovered her very unusual talent, she also found out that one of the few ways a person on the receiving end of this gift could die from it, was if he had a pacemaker.

"Most folks," her uncle told her later that night, "it just stuns 'em."

Uncle Frank thought about the situation for a moment and advised his niece to call 911. He said to tell them the truth all the way up to the point where her fingers turned into fireworks. At that point, Lilith and the truth were to part company. She was to tell them that the old man simply passed out half way down the hallway. He told his niece not to worry. He was on his way over and he would deal with what to tell the responding officers about her mother's absence, and why an eight-year-old girl was left to deal with the nasty neighbor on her own.

An ambulance arrived and two men removed the body from the hallway. Her mother was located, plied with coffee, and returned home. Then, Uncle Frank sat Lilith down and told her about her great-grandmother, and the unusual gift she had passed on to two of her children, one of her grandchildren, and now to Lilith.

It would be a number of years before Lilith fully understood how much more now stood between her and a dangerous world than just Dozer.

The meddlesome neighbor's death was ruled natural causes. That pacemaker of his just seized up from all the excitement it seemed, and he collapsed right there in the hallway of his neighbor's house. No one had any reason to question the coroner's ruling on the subject. Case closed.

As Lilith grew up and began learning how to control this newfound talent she had inherited from her great-grandmother, she discovered it came in handy quite nicely in high school when she began dating.

Lilith's mother was only seventeen years older than she was, and often borrowed her clothes. Once in her teens, Lilith knew exactly the kind of mother she didn't want to be. In fact, she wasn't sure she ever wanted to be a mother at all. The thought of passing down the sizzling fingers terrified her.

In her teens, the idea of aliens first began to enchant her. The notion was born that Lightning Fingers Lilith just might be an extraterrestrial herself. She found this possibility deliciously compelling.

She had learned how to control the charge just enough to cause a nasty shock if a boy got a little too "handsy" for her liking. She was usually able to laugh it off and convince the unsuspecting suitor that it was just static electricity from her blouse. A little elec-trocution always cooled overactive hormones down quickly.

Greg Bailey was the only boy who didn't buy that innocent explanation. During their senior year, his advances became a bit too ardent. When Lilith employed the finger trick, he jumped and asked her how she did that. When she floated the static electricity on the blouse story, he narrowed his eyes and looked at her for a long, cool moment. Then, he hesitantly reached out and ran his palm gently down the front of her sweater. Nothing happened.

"That's a neat parlor trick, Lil," he commented. "If you don't want to tell me how you did it, that's fine. But don't lie to me. That's just not cool."

They had been going out for nearly three months and Lilith was quite smitten with this young man. She had told him nearly everything about her life. He had even met her mother and taken her brothers to softball practice. She decided to try the truth on Greg to see how it fit. It would be the first time in the nine years since discovering what her fingers could do that she ever shared her secret with another living soul outside of her immediate family.

At first, Greg didn't believe her. But once she did a couple of visual demonstrations, he realized she was telling the truth. Greg recovered from his initial shock rather quickly—no pun intended. Then he laughed and kissed her fingertips, saying, "Well, I guess it's Lilith's way or the fry-way, huh?"

She laughed right along with him, quite relieved that he had taken it so well. However, she never told him about her neighbor turning into a life-size puppet and dropping dead in the hallway of her house. That was one story none of the Chalmers children would ever share—even with their spouses.

Lilith married Greg shortly after her eighteenth birthday. The marriage was a good one for the first few years, until Lilith's obsession with UFOs and extraterrestrials became nearly manic. It started with her founding the Rattlesnake UFO Club and holding monthly meetings in their home.

Wanting to support his wife, Greg never voiced his concern over her growing conviction that she herself was an alien. He believed eventually Lilith would outgrow such foolishness. He attended the meetings and tried his best not to laugh out loud at some of the off-the-wall theories and tales which were paraded out at these gatherings.

When the group grew too large to hold meetings in their apartment any longer, Lilith approached the church and asked about renting the meeting hall in the basement. Once they were moved there, Greg still attended the meetings with his wife. He did this mostly because he didn't like how some of the male members of this motley crew ogled her. Naturally, he didn't want those too-long glances to advance any further. With Greg present, no one would dare try to make a move on his Lilith. Greg was a big guy.

Eventually, when the group had grown to over twenty members, it was discussed, voted on, and decided by a show of hands that they would begin planning overnight stays in the desert out west to try and spot one of the elusive UFOs which held them so spellbound.

Some members claimed to have seen them already. There were two who were so unstable they scared even Lilith a little. The pair claimed to have met, travelled with, and been examined by actual extraterrestrials. Many of the members of the Rattlesnake

UFO club believed the stories of these alien encounters, but some were skeptical. On this Greg and Lilith were divided. She thought the encounters quite possible. Greg, on the other hand, thought it the insane ramblings of deeply troubled minds. They agreed to disagree, and Lilith began planning the first sojourn into the desert in search of a real life encounter of her own.

Greg went with Lilith on these weekend expeditions for the first few months. However, he quickly grew tired of the heat, the sticker bushes, and the mosquitos draining most of his blood. Eventually he stopped going with her, and shortly after that he quit attending the meetings all together.

The marriage began to show signs of strain. What had begun as his wife's charming little quirk had quickly spiraled into a virulent obsession—the earmarks of sheer madness looming just below the surface.

Greg wanted to turn the extra bedroom in their apartment into a nursery and begin making plans to start a family. Lilith, instead, turned it into her own personal UFO headquarters, complete with maps on the walls where areas of the most likely possible sightings were marked in red.

Lilith wrote countless blogs about the group's expeditions to the desert. She developed a following of like-minded people all over the world and became a sort of guru. Then she started printing flyers and leaflets about UFOs and their effects on mankind. She and her band of misfits passed them out all over town. They were everywhere. On the windshields of parked cars, in mailboxes, tacked up on telephone poles, and taped in store windows.

As the Rattlesnake UFO Club grew larger still, Lilith began to get a reputation which had nothing to do with her Daisy Duke shorts or her ample chest. This one was even worse. It was the *crazy lady* reputation. There is one in every small town, and Lilith was crowned Queen of the Cracked in her community.

She lost her job. When she finally told her husband she didn't want to have children, he dusted off the old joke about it being Lilith's way or the fry-way. With deep regret, he told her he guessed he'd be taking the fry-way after all.

Lilith was devastated and begged him to stay. He agreed to give the marriage one more try. His condition: she must dismantle the spare bedroom and put the UFO nonsense behind her.

She complied, but not for long. In the end, the call of the siren song in the desert out west was just too strong. The divorce was sad, quiet, and amicable.

Once Lilith had made her choice to follow the UFOs wherever they might lead and give herself fully to this single-minded quest, she was rewarded (if you can call it that) with the encounter she had been working toward for all these years. This happened during the Rattlesnake UFO Club's fortieth migration into the desert, just after three o'clock in the morning.

Now, we all know that nothing good ever happens at that ungodly hour, and the group's experience on this unforgettable night was no exception.

The craft was oblong in shape and maybe seven feet in diameter. It landed silently on three needle-thin legs. The legs were about four feet long and protruding from the thing's underbelly.

Tessa Winter was the first to become aware of it. She elbowed the snoring Roy Stark, who lay next to her in the tent. He awoke with a start. By then the others were stirring. The ship's lights were blinding. There looked to be hundreds of them aglow all over the body of the craft.

The group stood huddled together in a frightened knot and looked to their leader. Lilith was just as scared as her followers. She realized in all the years of searching she had really never believed this moment would come. At first it was just a novelty to label herself an extraterrestrial based on her unusual birthright. But now, here, in this hot, dry and very windy desert, she was faced with a reality she could not even comprehend.

She had spent five long years promoting this strange gospel to anyone who would listen. With nothing but the power of her convictions to guide her, she had sacrificed a good man, a good job, and a good life in the pursuit of this very event. But in her heart she never truly believed.

Lilith had absolutely no idea what to do. She stood as paralyzed as all of those looking to her for guidance.

When a door whirred to life before them and unfolded from the glowing vessel about twenty feet from where they stood, sheer chaos erupted. Everyone's paralysis broke at once. They turned to flee, tripping over one another in an effort to escape whatever was going to emerge from that unholy metal tank.

They made it about three yards before crashing into a pliable, invisible force field which had grown up around them. The force promptly began shrinking and herding them like sheep back in the direction they had come. It was like hitting a trampoline sideways.

They were trapped on all sides except the one which led back to the newcomer's vessel. An invisible power was propelling them in that direction. There was no fighting it.

And then the occupants of the ship in the desert emerged. And oh my! They were far more frightening than any of those assembled had ever envisioned.

Each member of the Rattlesnake UFO Club had dreamed of this encounter. But, nothing on this earth, or in their over-active imaginations, could ever have adequately prepared them for what now stood before them.

From the craft emerged three inhuman figures. They stood nearly eight feet tall, and their skin was transparent. Underneath their flesh, flowed and streamed silver. It was like looking inside a person and watching blood as it flowed through veins, only the blood was a metallic silver color. Impossibly long legs, feet clad in lace-up black work boots, arms with nearly human hands, and fingers that looked strong enough to crush bones to fine powder with the most casual of handshakes. The worst was their heads. Where their faces should have been, were large, square screens, each about four feet wide. They looked like plasma TVs.

Those screens mirrored the entire group where they stood frozen in horror. The Rattlesnake UFO Club had a panoramic view of each member's terrified face and trembling body—and it was in surround-sound. They not only saw themselves reflected on the three alien's face screens, but could also hear themselves through the speakers: Gasps, shouts, crying, all heard in Dolby quality high-def. Their terror echoed across the desert.

The aliens did not speak. The first one began to advance toward the Rattlesnake UFO Club. En-masse, they instinctively tried to back up. They collided with each other. Those in the rear fell against the force field and were propelled right back into those standing in front of them. The result was bedlam.

The screen on the marching creature's head suddenly changed. The group's picture disappeared, and was replaced by a close-up image of the youngest and smallest member of their party. It was Gloria Barber's twelve-year-old son, Russell.

When he saw his likeness staring back at him from the screen that served as the thing's face, the boy's bladder let go in a gush and he tried to hide behind his mother's shaking body. She instinctively stepped in front of him. Her terrified sobs reverberated from the speakers on the advancing creature's head.

As the monstrosity stomped through the sand and parted the group, heading directly for Russell with single-minded purpose, Lilith did the only thing she could think of. As it passed by her, she grabbed its arm with both hands and shot forth her special gift with everything she had.

When the sparks leapt from her fingers directly into the alien's skin, the screen atop its body changed again. The boy's picture vanished. His image was replaced by nothing but a pure wall of bloody scarlet. The Rattlesnake UFO Club was clearly seeing the extraterrestrial's shock and fury. From the speakers rang an ear-shattering scream of pain and rage that was eerily human.

The writhing creature tried to shake free of Lilith's grasp. She held fast and was lifted off the ground. Bare seconds later, the running silver beneath its skin began to bubble and turned dark red. The hideous thing's arm ignited in flames.

Lilith let go and landed in a graceless bundle at its feet. She covered her face against the baking heat, as the flames engulfed it. Arms flailing, feet back-peddling, it exploded, sending a mountain of shrapnel raining down on the group.

Several members received nasty cuts from falling pieces of screen that had once served as the odd being's head. More were burned as they were struck by smoldering alien body parts.

Later, they all agreed the injuries sustained were a small price to pay, when they considered what might have happened to Russell Barber had Lilith not kept her head. The story she told her followers was that she had "burned the alien with a lighter." They were all in a state of panic and their attention was on the advancing creature when Lilith made her move. None of them saw exactly what she had done. The lighter story was accepted without question. No one stopped to ponder just how flammable the huge creature must have been to become fully engulfed in flames by something as innocuous as the flick of a Bic.

Lilith knew none of the members of the Rattlesnake UFO Club would have wanted to learn the truth about how she had dispatched that walking freak show anyway. They had dealt with enough horror for one night without being introduced to her flammable fingers. One alien encounter for the evening was enough.

Seeing what had become of their comrade, the two remaining otherworldly visitors promptly retreated to the safety of their vessel and closed the hatch door. Mere seconds later, the ship roared to life and rose into the pre-dawn sky with frightening speed, retracting the amphibian-like legs beneath it. The force field vanished and those in the back of the group tumbled to the sand.

The members of the Rattlesnake UFO club, dazed and somber, tended to their wounded and hastily packed up their camp. They drove silently home, few having much to say. In the emergency room, sutures were applied and burns treated. The cover story told to the ER staff blamed the injuries on a nail-studded log in a campfire.

Lilith sustained the worst to her hands. It would be some time before she was able to use her special talent again, since all ten fingers ended the evening swaddled in bandages.

July 15th at the First Baptist Church was to be the Rattlesnake UFO Clubs final meeting. It was held one week after the incident in the desert.

Their numbers were smaller now. Many didn't need the closure of a farewell meeting. The occurrence out west had been enough for them. Noticeably absent was Gloria Barber, whose son had been the intended target of the strange extraterrestrial they met in the desert.

Gloria had lost a great many hours of sleep over the last week, wondering what would have become of her boy had Lilith not intervened. She had been permanently cured of her fascination with all things alien.

Lilith, at long last, had reached the end of her rope, too. She had spent the last week in terrible pain. And her hands weren't the worst of it. Her soul ached for all she had given up to achieve that grand-finale in the desert. She now realized none of it had been worth the sacrifice. One bitter, fateful night out west was all she needed to long for the life she had left behind. Lilith made the decision to not only disband the group, but the moment the Rattlesnake UFO club's final meeting was over, she intended to drive straight to Greg's house and plead with him for reconciliation. It was with great anticipation of that reunion when Lilith called the meeting to order.

She was unaware that outside, hovering about one hundred feet in the distance was a vessel. It was much larger than the one they had encountered out west the preceding week.

Just as the short meeting was preparing to adjourn, and the coffee pot was being rinsed, the huge craft landed in the church parking lot.

An entire alien army, consisting of literally dozens of soldiers, stood at the hatch as the vessel's door slid open. They were here to avenge the death of their captain.

Each one of the screens sitting atop the shoulders of those angry and grieving warriors bore the exact same image: A close-up of the pretty face of Lilith Chalmers.

THE DOGS OF RIVERVIEW ESTATES

AS THE REAL estate agent's car turned onto the street lined with neat little suburban homes, Laurel Davies thought the name of the development, Riverview Estates, was an awfully grand title for such a modest row of dwellings—the largest boasting 1600 square feet and a postage stamp back yard. And there was no view of any river that Laurel could see. Just a tiny body of water that looked more like a creek running behind the foliage at the back of the houses.

When Laurel questioned the realtor about the river's diminutive size, she replied, "Don't let it fool you. You could hide a good sized body in there if someone was unfortunate enough to fall in."

As they pulled to a stop in front of the "For Sale" sign, Laurel smiled at two young girls playing jacks at the curb next door. They raised their hands in a wave and returned to their game. Laurel took in the cozy little blue house with white shutters. The lawn was freshly mowed and dotted with a few stray fall leaves. Two planter boxes flanked the porch with rich pink and yellow flowers. A warm feeling spread through her stomach, as the words *this could be the one* popped into her mind.

Laurel tuned out the realtor's endless monologue about how she must move quickly because there was another couple interested in making an offer, and this gem wouldn't last long. The real estate agent launched into the same speech with every house she had shown Laurel—and there had been many.

Laurel walked slowly through the small home. She began mentally placing her furniture in the two bedrooms and tiny alcove that the contractor stuck a set of double doors on and generously called a den. She inspected the kitchen and smiled appreciably.

The cabinets were painted a soft butter-yellow. There was a bright eating area nestled in the corner, bathed in afternoon sunlight. Laurel envisioned drinking her morning coffee in that sunbathed nook and knew this was home.

No one was very surprised that at twenty-seven and still single, Laurel had purchased her first home. She had always been a very practical girl. The real surprise was that she was still single. While she may have been very judicious, Laurel was also very pretty and never lacked for suitors. The honey colored hair and trim figure she inherited from her mother—the financial acumen was all her dad. Laurel graduated college with a BA in finance. Before the ink was even dry on her diploma she went to work for a prestigious accounting firm, and had been there for the last five years. She was educated, financially savvy, and knew how to budget. Once she was approved for the home loan she began her search, anxious to be able to call something her own, and as she told her mother, "paint the bathroom hot pink if the mood strikes me."

That had been six months ago, and nothing within her modest budget caught Laurel's fancy until the blue house at the far corner of Riverview Estates.

Her boyfriend was a local policeman named Brian Parker. He installed a motion sensor light by the driveway and another in the backyard the day before she moved in. The street was dimly lit, with only one street lamp on the narrow road. Laurel was grateful to have the extra light Brian had so thoughtfully put in for her. As her mother was always reminding her, "A girl alone can never be too careful."

Of course she wasn't completely alone. There was Brian. While the relationship was relatively young, so far things were going very well. The pair had been set up on a blind date by friends three months before. It was a pleasant surprise to discover a connection, both immediate and intense. The romance moved quickly and they had been together ever since.

Laurel moved in to her new home on a rainy Saturday morning. On that first night, weary with exhaustion, she fell into bed amid the sea of unpacked boxes and immediately drifted to sleep. Several hours later, what sounded to Laurel's tired mind like dozens of barking dogs woke her up. Judging by the rich, baritone timbre of the constant baying, these were no small dogs. In fact, they sounded positively huge. She glanced at the glowing green numerals on the clock by the bed and read 1:34 AM.

"Great," she muttered, rolling onto her side and pulling the pillow over her head. "One of the neighbors is running a kennel."

Overcome by exhaustion, she eventually fell back asleep in spite of the ceaseless canine symphony taking place nearby.

Laurel didn't hear the dogs again for several days, and she forgot all about them. She had more important things on her mind at this point. For instance, why a mutual acquaintance called her at work to tell her he saw Brian out with a pretty redhead at a roadhouse on the edge of town a few days before.

When she asked her boyfriend about it, he flatly denied the accusation, but he wouldn't meet her eyes. Because Laurel didn't want to consider the possibility that Brian could possibly be unfaithful to her, she chose to believe him and let it go.

The next weekend the dogs woke her again. This time it was after three o'clock in the morning. Laurel donned a bathrobe and slippers and stepped onto her front porch. Once outside, the chorus of barking was incredibly loud. It seemed to be coming in surround-sound from the very heavens above, enveloping the darkness from everywhere and nowhere all at the same time. It was impossible to gauge which direction it originated from. It could have come from anywhere, including her half-asleep imagination, she supposed. She walked cautiously up the street a few feet, under the curious eye of some unknown nocturnal bird sitting perched on the lone street lamp up ahead.

When the sound of the dogs reached nearly earsplitting intensity, Laurel fled back inside her house and shut the door against the cold night air and the overpowering thunder of what sounded like dozens of very large hellhounds. She was reminded of the three headed variety she had once read about in a mythology book.

Sleep didn't come easy again that night, but when slumber did finally wrap Laurel in its arms, the dogs quieted.

In the morning Laurel's unease still held. Over a cup of coffee in her sunny kitchen she puzzled over why the dogs sounded as though they were coming from all around her. Why it felt like their other-worldly caterwaul was issuing from the very earth itself. With a shudder, she chided herself a fool, and said out loud, "More likely coming from your own mind, you ninny. It's a well-known fact that in the middle of the night everything is amplified. Especially my imagination."

She decided to broach the subject of the dogs with her neighbor, Carol. She was the mother of the two little girls Laurel had seen playing when she first came to look at the house.

"Carol," Laurel asked, "Am I imagining things or does someone nearby own several large dogs? They sure bark a lot at night."

Her neighbor laughed nervously and said, "Well, at least it's a safe neighborhood."

"So, I'm not crazy. Who do they belong to, and why don't I ever hear them during the day?" Laurel pressed.

"Do you know we haven't had a break-in or a car prowl here in years," the woman answered, dodging the question altogether. She gave Laurel an encouraging smile.

"I'm not saying I want to cause trouble, I would just like to know who owns them. How many are there?"

The woman sighed. She took Laurel by the elbow and led her to the sofa. "I can see you aren't going to let this go. You better sit down."

A puzzled frown creased Laurel's brow. "What's going on?" she asked, bewildered.

Carol sat down beside her and began, "Well, you aren't going to believe this—new people never do, but the dogs belong to Riverview Estates—to all of us."

Laurel nodded, "Okay, so whose house do they live at? Who takes care of them?"

A pained expression came onto Carol's face, "I don't know, honey. No one has ever actually seen them—well, that's not entirely true. When little Bobby Ketchum got into his dad's heart pills last August, his mom heard one of them scratching on the door so loud it woke her up from her nap. She thinks she might have seen it for a second when she got up, but she was never sure. They reached the hospital in time, and that's the important thing. The kid could have died if the dogs hadn't woken her up that day."

Laurel smiled an indulgent smile—the kind reserved for the mentally unstable and potentially dangerous. Rising from the couch, she said, "I see. Okay, well thanks, I should probably get going…"

"I told you, you wouldn't believe me," Carol said, a small, sad smile on her lips.

"Well, you have to admit, it's a little tough to swallow, these phantom dogs of yours."

"Not mine. All of ours," Carol replied, "Someday you might be glad we have them around."

Laurel returned to her house to call Brian and see what he would make of this, but her message light was blinking, and she never got around to calling him to talk about the odd conversation with Carol. After she listened to the message, phantom dogs were the last thing on her mind.

The message was from her friend Chloe. She said she ran into Brian last night at a local restaurant. He was out with a redhead, and took great pains to hide the woman behind his back when Chloe approached the couple at the bar.

Laurel, in her practical, no-nonsense way, was no longer willing to ignore the rumors. She drove straight to Brian's apartment across town. He kept a spare key under a potted plant on the porch. Brian had told her she could use the key any time. Laurel thought the fact that Brian had shared the location of his house key with her was a major milestone in their relationship—a rite of passage even. Of course, she also knew that when he said she could use it "any time," loosely translated, that meant when they were meeting at his apartment for a date and she arrived before he was off work, or perhaps emergencies. *Close enough,* Laurel thought. *Rumors of a redhead constitute an emergency in my opinion.*

She walked in on Brian and the now famous redhead in an advanced state of undress, then turned around and walked back out. Tears blurred her vision as she ran to her car.

Buckling his pants, Brian ran after her yelling, "I can explain! This isn't what it looks like."

But practical Laurel knew there was no explanation, and it was exactly what it looked like. She was done with Brian Parker for good.

Laurel was completely heartbroken. Like her house, when she met Brian, she thought he might just be *the one.* She went to bed certain she would die in her sleep, choking on her own sorrow.

She took a sleeping pill, determined not to be awakened by her broken heart or any dogs, phantom or otherwise.

In the wee hours of the night Laurel roused briefly, but remained mostly cocooned in drug-induced slumber. She felt a comforting warmth pressing against her side. What felt like a sandpapery tongue licked the drying tears from her cheeks. She drifted off again, one arm draped loosely over the furry presence lying beside her in bed. By morning she had convinced herself it was all a sleeping pill-induced dream. The only thing she couldn't explain were the few wiry, black hairs she found clinging to the coverlet.

On Monday, Laurel found Brian waiting by her car when she got off work. She told him to leave her alone and tried to push past him. He blocked her from getting into the car and grabbed her arm.

"Laurel, I messed up. I know that. Babe, please just give me another chance," he begged.

"No. It's over, Brian. Let go of me!" She tried to pull away from his grasp and his fingers tightened painfully into her flesh.

"Ow, you're hurting me," she cried.

People were starting to notice. Brian looked around guiltily and dropped her arm.

"This isn't over, Laurel," he spat, his voice lowered to a menacing whisper. Then he stormed off across the parking lot.

Laurel was rattled by Brian's violent outburst and felt even more resolve to end their relationship. She'd never seen him behave like that before.

She arrived home to numerous messages on her answering machine. Some begging her to take him back, others threatening that "she'd be sorry" if she didn't.

She deleted the messages and cried herself to sleep.

Sometime in the middle of the night, Laurel was awakened. It wasn't the strange canine melody this time. She heard something crash against the back of her house. Terrified, she rose on unsteady legs and switched on the bedroom light. When she looked out the window, the motion sensor light was on and bits of broken glass twinkled on the patio. She ran to her living room and saw the sliding door leading to the backyard shattered. Glass littered the carpet and there was a brick lying amid the shards. Laurel immediately called 911. Two officers showed up not long after to take a report. One of them was Brian.

He acted with professional indifference as he filled out the police report and taped up the gaping hole in her door. She was too frightened to mention anything to the other officer about who she believed might be responsible for the vandalism. How could she tell him, when the suspect was standing in her kitchen writing the report?

The following two weeks were among the worst of Laurel's life. They were wrought with terror. Several times she woke up in the night convinced she heard noises. Twice the motion sensor lights were illuminated and she couldn't fall back asleep. However, several times she would wake to find the lights had not been activated and it was all in her mind. That didn't stop her from worrying over the other two occasions. Something or someone had tripped those lights. With bitter irony, she imagined the very man who had installed them slinking through her backyard and peering in the windows while she slept. She was becoming a nervous wreck.

During those weeks the dogs remained silent, but Brian did not. His harassing phone calls were endless and making her life a living hell. She changed her phone number and made sure it was unlisted. Because he was a police officer, Brian easily obtained the new number. The calls continued without so much as a pause. In exasperation, Laurel unplugged the phone.

Brian's behavior escalated. Flowers were left on her doorstep. Then notes, gifts, candy. Anything to generate some reaction. She ignored it all and threw everything in the trash.

Brian began parking across the street and watching her when she left work. He followed her when she went out. She would come out of the grocery store or the pharmacy and see him parked in the lot, watching. Sometimes even in his patrol car.

The night she came home and found a dead bird, ashen as a tomb, in a gift box on her doorstep, she called the police again. This time she told the dispatcher not to send Officer Parker and explained why.

Another officer, another report. When Laurel told the policeman who she thought was behind it, he laughed and said, "You gotta be kidding. Brian Parker? Look, lady, I'm not trying to hurt your feelings or anything, but he's already seeing someone else. I don't think he's so torn up about your break-up that he'd be pulling these kinds of pranks. Remember, he is still a cop."

Laurel had never been so frightened in her life. This was Brian's friend and coworker she was trying to convince, and she knew whose side he was on. If the police refused to believe her, she was in serious trouble. Brian Parker was the department's fair-haired boy, and no one was going to even look into the possibility that he could be stalking her. That left her completely vulnerable to anything he might do.

On a drizzly, gray Sunday she sat on her front steps crying. Mrs. Flannel, the elderly woman across the street, trudged up the walk carrying a plate of cookies. She looked exactly the part of your favorite grandma, straight out of central casting. Her long gray hair was tightly coiled in a bun. She wore a house dress, cotton stockings and sensible shoes. "I saw you from my kitchen window. Thought you could use some cheering up."

Laurel wiped at her streaming eyes with the heels of her hands.

Mrs. Flannel smoothed her house dress and sat down beside Laurel on the steps. "Have a cookie, dear."

Laurel smiled her thanks and popped one into her mouth.

"Do you want to talk about it?" the old woman asked kindly.

"I think my ex-boyfriend threw a brick through my back door and left a dead bird on the doorstep. He's stalking me," Laurel told her neighbor.

"Have you called the police?" the woman asked.

"He is the police," Laurel answered. Frustrated tears filled her eyes again. "They don't believe me."

Mrs. Flannel was quiet for a moment. She said, "Don't worry, honey. The dogs won't let anyone hurt you. Not even a cop."

Laurel rolled her eyes. There it was again. The mystery dogs of Riverview Estates. "Mrs. Flannel, what's the deal with those dogs? Where are they?"

The woman was quiet for so long that Laurel didn't think she was going to answer. Finally she handed Laurel another cookie and sighed. "Let me tell you a little story."

Laurel took the cookie and nodded for the old woman to go on.

"There was a man who lived next door to your house—the one Carol and Bill own now. His name was Allen Ludlow. Oh, this was maybe twenty or twenty-five years ago I would say. Allen was an assistant district attorney with the state. He prosecuted a very nasty group of men who were running some type of dog-fighting ring. These were horrible people. When they were arrested, the authorities found eight or nine dogs being kept in miserable conditions in cages. No one could go near them because they were vicious. They had been bred to fight from the time they were puppies. There was talk of shooting them. They were not only wounded and malnourished, but quite dangerous, so no one would adopt them. If they had been brought to a shelter they would have been put to sleep, so Allen took them all in and gave them a home. He built individual kennels for them and nursed them back to health. Eventually, with good care and gentleness he domesticated the dogs."

Laurel nodded sympathetically. "He sounds like a wonderful person, but that was a long time ago. What does it have to do with the barking I hear now? And where is Mr. Ludlow? Did he move away?"

Mrs. Flannel shook her head sadly. "No, sweetie. Mr. Ludlow died about six years ago."

"Did he keep all the dogs or did he find homes for them once they were domesticated?" Laurel asked.

Mrs. Flannel smiled. "He kept all of them except one. He gave Bruno, a Pit-bull, to the Millers'. They were the couple who owned your house."

"Why did he give them the dog?"

"Well, you see, the neighborhood had been experiencing a rash of break-ins. It was really quite frightening. Usually no one was home when the crimes occurred, but on the night the Millers' house was hit, unfortunately, they were inside. The intruder tied them both up and held a knife to their throats. God knows what would have happened if Bruno hadn't broken through the fence and found a way into their house. He attacked the burglar and barked like crazy until he woke half the neighborhood. He even managed to hold the thief there until police arrived. He was quite an amazing dog. After that, Mrs. Miller asked Allen if they could adopt Bruno. He lived right in your house for thirteen years. He's buried beneath that beautiful rose bush you have in the back yard. The robberies all stopped after that incident. And no crime has been committed in Riverview ever since. The dogs still look out for the neighborhood, and Bruno will always look after whoever lives in your house. You may not believe that now, but I think someday you will."

Laurel thanked the old woman for telling her the story. She wasn't sure how much of the tale was truth, and how much was small-town lore, mingled with a touch of senility, but it was certainly an interesting story.

As she rose to go inside the house, Laurel said, "I hope Bruno will forgive me, but I am still going to keep my appointment with the alarm company to have a security system installed tomorrow."

Mrs. Flannel smiled knowingly. "Honey, you do whatever makes you feel better. But trust me, you are safe here."

The glowing numbers on the bedside clock read 4:21 AM. There was shouting. The voice, too muffled to be understood, woke Laurel with a start. She threw off the covers, scared half out of her mind. She looked out the back window where she thought the sound was coming from and squinted into the gloom, but could see nothing. There was only blackness beyond her window. The motion sensor light remained dark. A minute later the commotion had shifted. It was now coming from the direction of her living room.

Laurel, too scared to turn on the light, groped in the dark until she found the phone. She lifted the receiver in one trembling hand to call 911 and heard nothing. She depressed the hook twice, but couldn't get a dial tone. The telephone line had been cut.

Cringing in the corner, Laurel heard the unmistakable sound of a dog growling. It was followed by a deep and ominous whine, coming from the back of the throat of a dog simply too huge to be imagined. Then there were three sharp barks, so loud they sounded like gun shots.

Laurel distinctly heard a male's voice. *Brian? Is it Brian?* her terrified mind wailed.

The voice sounded frightened. There was a sharp intake of breath, the ripping of cloth, and then a horrified yell. "Get away from me. Ah God, let go, let go!" This was followed by a loud thunk and a bloodcurdling scream.

The world swam gray before Laurel. Succumbing to the terror, she slid to the floor in a dead faint. When she woke it was light outside.

On trembling legs she slunk into the living room. The back door stood half open, the curtain blowing restlessly in the breeze. Laurel tentatively peered out the door. She saw broken glass lying on the patio. The motion sensor light Brian had installed was shattered.

Apart from the broken light nothing appeared amiss. As she turned to go into the kitchen, Laurel spied a piece of blue cloth lying on the carpet. She picked it up and gasped when she realized what it was.

Brian's police uniforms all had his last name neatly embroidered at the left breast in fine script. On the fabric she held were the letters *ark* and half an *e* in gold stitching. Her gaze shifted to the kitchen and her eyes widened in alarm. There was a small puddle of what appeared to be blood on the floor. It was followed by a few dime sized droplets. Laurel gingerly put her fingers to one of the blood spatters and they came away tacky. She fought a wave of dizziness and struggled not to pass out again. The blue cloth with the embroidered letters fluttered out of her hand and she grabbed the counter to keep from falling.

Once she felt steady again, Laurel went out to her back yard. She walked to the far edge of her property and looked out into the dense foliage behind the house. About a foot from the edge of the river she saw an abandoned shoe. Working her way carefully through the thorny overgrowth, Laurel encountered another piece of blue cloth impaled on a tree limb. It was larger than the piece she had found inside the house. She plucked it off the branch and folded it into her hand. At the water's edge she looked curiously at the mist rising off the river. She couldn't recall ever seeing a haze quite like that over the water before. The morning was quiet, the air unnaturally still. Laurel stood for a moment listening to the sound of the insects in the grass and the birds in the trees. She picked up the shoe and recognized it at once. The black, patent leather lace-up was standard issue, and worn by all the town's patrolmen. The realtor's words echoed in her ear, "You could hide a good sized body in there…"

Like, oh, say a six-foot tall policeman for instance? Laurel wondered. She was suddenly calm. She felt the tension leave her shoulders and something loosen in her chest. The nightmare was finally over.

She pulled in a long, cleansing breath of fresh morning air and carried the shoe back into the house along with the recovered piece of fabric.

By evening it was all over the news that a police officer had gone missing. His patrol car was found about a half mile from Riverview Estates, but the officer never returned from his shift last night. It was a quiet night and no one tried to reach him by radio for the last couple hours he was on duty, so they didn't know he was missing until he failed to return to the station at the end of his shift.

Laurel was questioned. She told the officers nothing about the events which took place just before dawn, nor did she mention the blood in her kitchen or the items found near the river.

In the still of the night, just after midnight, Laurel sat up in bed and turned on the lamp. She said to the empty room, "You know, the drink might not be that deep. I think the realtor exaggerated about that. They may still find him."

In the quiet house, two immediate and reassuring barks echoed off the walls in answer.

Satisfied, Laurel nodded. "Okay. As long as you're sure. Goodnight, Bruno," she said, extinguishing the light and going back to sleep.

Brian Parker was never found.

The following summer a young couple moved in across the street. A week after they arrived, the woman cautiously asked Laurel about barking dogs she heard in the middle of the night. Laurel told her, "Well, you aren't going to believe this—new people never do, but the dogs belong to Riverview Estates—to all of us."

BONUS STORY

RETURN TO BELLA LUNA: A COSTLY AFFAIR

Foreword

Well, you've come this far, so I hope you will stay just a little bit longer and read the tenth tale—a bonus story.

Those of you who read my second book, "Be Careful What You Wish For," will probably remember a few of the people on the following pages. I hope you will enjoy running into these old friends again as much as I did. Who could forget Hollywood actress, Stormie Banks? To this day, she is still the character I had the most fun creating, and her story among the most compelling I ever had the pleasure of writing.

If you are unfamiliar with the book, it is a trilogy that centers around a bookstore in Seattle. Belda, the strange old woman who owns the shop, offers the unique service of creating potions that make people's dreams come true—not always with the most pleasant of consequences.

I have been asked a few times if I ever plan to write a sequel to that book. Though at this time I don't have plans for a sequel, I did find that I wasn't quite done visiting the drafty old bookstore just yet. There were still one or two customers who had a story to tell and they beckoned me back for a short visit.

If you have already read "Be Careful What You Wish For" you will probably enjoy stopping by Bella Luna again and scratching Eros under the chin. If you haven't, you might find wandering the shop for the first time rather fascinating. There is always a hot cup of tea and some unique and intriguing items for sale at Bella Luna—though you may have to ask the staff to help you find them. Not everything they offer can be found on the shelves.

I hope your brief visit will inspire you to pick up a copy of the book and get to know the people you meet on the next few pages just a little bit better.

Krystal Lawrence
April 2016
Seattle, WA

Part I: The Judge

THERE WAS A chill in the air as the well-dressed woman closed the door against the damp October day. Hearing the bell resonate its melodic tune above the door, Gabriella turned to face the new customer. She smiled warmly. "Good afternoon. Welcome to Bella Luna. Is there something I can help you find?"

The woman bore the nervous posture and darting eyes Gabriella had witnessed on many others patrons before her. She was clearly not here to browse the bookstore, but had come for the other service offered within the walls of the dusty old shop.

Gabriella heard the floorboards creak above and a moment later the door to Belda's apartment opened. Eros, Belda's black cat, descended the staircase ahead of his mistress and jumped on the counter next to Gabriella. The smartly dressed lady softened at once and reached out to scratch Eros under his chin.

As Gabriella introduced the cat, Belda began her slow laborious trek to the bottom of the staircase. Her arthritis pained her terribly, and today was not one of her better days. Gabriella was surprised to see her at all. She clearly wanted to meet the new patron in person.

Though Gabriella had taken over making the potions a few years before, Belda had the uncanny knack of always knowing

241

when she needed to take care of a customer personally. Clearly this lady was someone of importance.

Reaching the bottom of the staircase at last, Belda extended her misshapen hand to the woman. "Gabby, dear, please brew a pot of tea—my special blend. This is Judge Vargas. I will be taking care of her myself today."

"Right away, Belda," Gabriella replied, turning on her heel to go tend to the tea.

Belda took Mrs. Vargas's elbow and led her to the small office in the back of the shop where they met with clients.

Once settled in the chairs of the stifling room with two steaming mugs of tea before them, the woman said, "As I told you when I called, my friend Laurel Wainright gave me your name. Laurel and I go way back. She was the maid of honor at my wedding. Lord, that was a long time ago." The woman sighed forlornly. "Laurel said you helped her with a personal problem. When her husband was…uh, when he got himself in some trouble last year."

"I am acquainted with Mrs. Wainright. She's a lovely lady," Belda replied neutrally and sipped her tea. "I'm afraid I don't discuss my clients or their business with anyone, Judge Vargas."

The woman barked an anxious laugh and her hands fluttered nervously in her lap. "No, of course not. And please, call me Francine. Judge sounds so formal. You probably know I am not on the bench anymore."

Belda looked deeply into the woman's eyes and held her gaze long enough that Francine Vargas looked down uncomfortably.

Finally Belda said, "Why don't we talk about you, Francine. What is it that brings you to Bella Luna today? Seattle is a long way from Washington DC."

"This is very difficult for me." Tears sprang to her eyes.

Belda nodded reassuringly and pointed one gnarled finger at the woman's teacup. "Why don't you drink up? You may find it a little easier to discuss the issue which brought you so many miles once you have been warmed by the tea."

"Yes, alright." The woman's eyes locked on Belda's and went blank. She began breathing more shallowly and drank greedily from the steaming mug. A few moments later she placed the mug on the table beside her and blotted her lips demurely with a napkin.

"My husband is having an affair," Francine Vargas began unceremoniously.

Belda said nothing.

"Of course, that's not really the problem. He has had many of them over the years." Francine grimaced bitterly.

"If your husband's extra-marital dalliance is not the trouble, then what is?" Belda asked gently.

"Ted can usually untangle himself once he has had his fill of whoever the hussy-de jour is. This time is different. We are getting close to starting an aggressive campaign—one I have been waiting thirty years for. I am not going to have some stupid Hollywood bimbo with fake tits larger than her IQ screw the whole thing up."

"I see." Belda nodded. "And how can I help?"

"I want you to fix it," Francine cried desperately. "I didn't stay married to that bastard for over half my life just to watch him throw away our entire future for one of his sluts. Can you take care of it? You know…like you did when Chad Wainright was whoring around?"

Belda's eyes narrowed. "Take care of it how?"

Francine sighed. "Look, if this thing gets out, it's all over. Ted's political career is finished. My plan is to live in the Whitehouse, not in the pages of some stinking tabloid. Do you understand?"

"So, you are here because you want me to prevent your husband's affair from becoming front page news?" Belda asked.

"Keeping it away from the media is only part of it. I need this bitch neutralized before she ruins my entire future." Francine spat venomously. "Can you do that?"

"You say this woman is in Hollywood. Is she an actress?" Belda crinkled her brow in distaste.

Francine nodded.

"Is she well-known?"

"Very."

"So any ill fate which might befall her would make headlines of its own, would it not?" Belda enquired.

Francine hesitated. "Does that matter?" she asked.

Belda shrugged. "It complicates things."

"So what are you saying? You won't do it, or it's just going to cost me more? I didn't figure getting rid of the goddamn blow-up doll was going to come cheap."

"It is not the money that concerns me. We will discuss the financial aspect of our arrangement later. First, I need you to answer one question."

"What is it?" Francine looked nervously at Belda and then shot her eyes sideways.

"Do you want your husband's mistress dead?"

Francine flinched as though she had just been struck. When she hesitated to answer, Belda said, "I only ask because the word neutralized can mean a number of things. In order to help you I need to know exactly the resolution you are seeking."

Francine looked at Belda for a long moment before slowly nodding her head. "It's the only way to insure she won't cause further problems down the road." She quickly added, "I can pay whatever you want. Just get rid of Margo Lovegood and make sure their filthy affair dies with her. No one must ever find out about it."

"Very well, Francine. I will help you. However, there are a few matters we need to discuss first. It appears Mrs. Wainright may have been a bit indiscreet when she spoke of my services. Did she also mention my terms?"

Francine smiled bitterly. "You are referring to the punishment should I tell anyone about our arrangement? Yes, she explained that it would cost me my life."

Belda looked deeply into the woman's eyes. "And you agree to this?"

Francine nodded without hesitation. "Let me explain something. There are many people who dream of becoming president before the ink is even dry on their law degree. My dream was a little different when I graduated Yale. I never aspired to be a politician. I wanted to see the visions I had for this country materialize without having to sell my soul to the devil. You might argue that is what I am doing now, of course. But back then, what I dreamed of—what I still dream of—is having the power to change and ultimately enhance this nation without engaging in all the bribery and trickery that goes along with political life."

Belda looked thoughtful. "A noble goal. May I ask how you expect to accomplish it without taking on the mantle of president yourself?"

"The First Lady wields tremendous influence over her husband's decisions. She has as much power over policy making, if not more, than her husband does. Only she gets to keep her hands clean. You see, I knew from the day I met Ted that someday he was destined to be president. You could say that was really the chief quality I was looking for in a potential mate. Before you feel too sorry for Ted, you should know that he wasn't looking for love either. He was looking for a young woman with the proper education, bloodline and social standing to be the optimum First Lady. We had an unspoken understanding. We knew that together, one day we could seize the Whitehouse."

"I can't believe your marriage was based entirely on political ambition. Surely his infidelity has caused you pain over the years?" Belda wondered.

Francine shrugged. "I knew what I was getting myself into. The quest for power can be much more intoxicating than romance. At least it was for me. I wanted to change the world. I still do. In order to achieve that kind of authority without compromising my morality I knew I would have to marry a very influential and driven person. One who wouldn't mind sacrificing his soul for absolute power. I was willing to give up love if I could reach the Whitehouse with my own integrity intact. Unfortunately, because I have to clean up his mess, my husband has forced me to give that up, too. After everything this has cost me, if I can't be First Lady my life isn't worth a damn anyway. So, the answer to your question is yes. I accept your terms to eliminate Margo Lovegood."

Belda quoted Francine Vargas the price for her services, and thought, *Oh hell! Not another actress.*

After seeing Francine Vargas out of the shop, Belda asked Gabriella to text Nicholas. She had an errand for him to run. Apparently Laurel Wainright had forgotten the terms of the agreement she entered into with Belda when she requested her help last year. Sometimes their customers needed a little gentle reminder of just what could happen if they talked too much.

Part II: The Actress

Underneath a tight chignon, held in place by half a can of hairspray, stood the poised figure of a shapely woman in a low-cut evening gown. She flashed a thousand megawatt smile for the cameras and pirouetted to show the back of her ridiculously expensive designer dress. Her hair did not move even a fraction of an inch during this maneuver. Nor did her impressive breasts, which were secured by about a yard of gravity-defying tape.

Waiting behind Margo Lovegood loomed an impossibly handsome man; her date for tonight's event. He stood a respectful, non-spotlight-stealing distance behind the actress. Once the photographers had their way with her, Margo took the arm of the gentleman she referred to as tonight's arm candy and entered the auditorium for the award show. She was one of the evening's Best Actress nominees. This was not the first time. A cabinet in her living room was lined with various awards.

There was still a little time before the cameras would begin rolling and the comedian hosting the show would jog on stage and begin his opening monologue. Margo excused herself from the VIP table and went in search of a ladies room, where she could snort a little happy dust in private.

She hated these things. The blow was the only way she could even make it through the night in towering high-heels that pinched her feet, itchy tape wound tightly about her midsection, and an uncomfortable dress she would need Houdini to help her get out of later. She often wondered if the public understood the price celebrities paid to look fabulous. Then again, she supposed for the multi-million dollar paychecks her movies paid, she could suffer through one uncomfortable evening every now and then.

After sitting through an hour and a half of the droning award show, Margo's category was at last being awarded. Though she had predicted the outcome, Margo acted surprised and humble when her name was pulled from the envelope. This was her third win for Best Actress.

She kissed her date, teetered onto the stage and tearfully thanked all the correct people. Margo politely stopped talking when the symphony cut her off.

She sat through the rest of the seemingly endless night, and then posed for more pictures before finally escaping the arm candy and the rest of the pretty people.

Knowing how short the shelf-life was on a leading lady, Margo intended to stay Hollywood's darling for as long as she possibly could. She would show up for these evenings, pose on the red carpet and smile for the cameras until she could no longer pull in the several-million dollar price tag for a role. Then she would retire. She had little interest in ever playing second fiddle. The first time someone dared try and cast her in a supporting role she would pack up and leave Hollywood for good, vowing never to truss up her aching boobs in straight jacket-like tape again.

She couldn't stand the place anyway. She hated all the plastic people, and was well aware that most of her "friends" were only in her life because throwing around her name got them tables in over-booked restaurants and put them at the front of the line at trendy nightclubs. They all hoped a small bit of her fame and fortune would rub off on them. The day she stopped being offered the choice roles was the same day all those lovely friends would stop taking her phone calls and wander off to sniff out the next big star like bloodhounds.

Everyone except Ted. Ted loved her for who she was, not what she was.

Instead of going to the after-parties with all the other A-listers, Margo Lovegood went to a Beverly Hills hotel known for its discretion and waited for the politician. He should have been home with his wife in Washington DC, but was instead in California to celebrate Margo's latest victory.

The affair had been going strong for over a year, and Margo was growing tired of Ted Vargas's repeated assurances that he would leave his wife.

There was currently quite a lot of talk circulating about Ted having his eye set on the Whitehouse in the next election. If this was true, Margo knew Ted would never leave his marriage, despite his promises to the contrary.

He was a third-term Democratic senator in a mostly red state in the South. He was popular, well-liked by both parties, and stood a good chance of being nominated if he went for the gold. There was a Super PAC waiting in the wings with many heavy-hitters willing to foot the bill for Ted's campaign. Pharmaceutical and environmental lobbyists alike had him in their back pocket, as did the NRA. He was a Democrat walking around in a Republican suit,

spouting just enough bible-speak to keep the conservatives capti-
vated, and just enough global warming babble to keep the left
firmly on his side. Both parties adored him.

His wife had the perfect pedigree for First Lady. Schooled at
Vassar, and later graduating summa cum laude from Yale,
Francine Vargas was the youngest woman ever appointed as a fed-
eral court judge. She sat on the bench until she retired early at
fifty-six, so she could devote herself full-time to her husband's political ambitions. Their only son was in his third year of law school
at Harvard. Ted's future looked good.

During a previous presidential election he was asked to be the
running mate of the Democratic hopeful. Having superior instincts,
Ted turned him down. A wise decision, as his party lost that
election.

He took the next eight years to ingratiate himself in
Washington and cultivate a bi-partisan network of adoring fans.
He kept a precise accounting of every favor granted, fully intending
to call them in later when campaign contributions and endorse-
ments were needed.

Thus far, Ted Vargas had managed to defy all the laws of political gravity by not getting caught, quite literally, with his pants
down. His past could very easily come back to haunt him. Margo
was not the first woman he had been involved with over the years.
In fact, there were dozens. Ted was an extremely charismatic and
persuasive man. He always picked his extra-marital dalliances
wisely and cautiously. Most were well known figures like himself.
Ladies who stood to lose just as much as he did should an affair
become public.

Only twice did Ted ever stray with anonymous women— those
who might seek to benefit from a scandalous relationship being
leaked to the press. Predictably, both asked for huge pay-offs when

Ted chose to end his relationship with them. They both disappeared under mysterious circumstances shortly after voicing their demands.

Margo Lovegood was the only woman who had ever pressured Ted to leave his wife. She didn't seem to care about the impact on her career the affair could have. She also didn't care about his political aspirations. She was a woman very used to getting whatever she wanted—and what she wanted most was to be Ted's wife. It astounded him that Margo could actually believe such a scenario was anywhere in the realm of possibility.

When she had first broached the subject of Ted divorcing Francine, he readily agreed. He wasn't thinking clearly at the calculated moment she chose to bring up such a taboo topic. In that instant, had Margo asked him to make her his running mate in the upcoming election, he would have not only promised to do so, he would have ordered campaign buttons and assured her it was a brilliant idea. Right then, Ted Vargas would have agreed to give Margo anything. You see, Margo's naked body was a breathtaking sight to behold. There wasn't a man alive who could resist her charms, no matter how high the price. When presented with such glorious temptation the word "no" ceased to exist in Ted's vocabulary.

This was how he currently found his political ambitions doused in gasoline, with Margo standing over them holding a lit match.

That rash promise to walk out on his marriage had been months ago, and Ted had been stalling her ever since. He could not very well tell Margo the only reason he agreed to a divorce was because she was in the process of seducing him at the exact moment she presented the idea. As time went by he continued to offer numerous false assurances that he would leave his wife any day now.

Those blatant lies were now catching up with him. Election season was right around the corner, and Margo had grown weary of his promises. Ted's hopes of her tiring of the relationship and replacing him with one of the pretty-boy actors she wore on her arm like jewelry at the awards shows were futile. Thinly veiled threats were being whispered in his ear. They hinted toward a very public tantrum she may just decide to throw during the primaries if she didn't get her way. A tantrum she would insure was heard around the globe.

Ted knew a scandal like that would not only be political suicide for him, it could potentially ruin his son's future, too. Not to mention the cost of a messy divorce.

Ted was growing desperate. He was considering resorting to drastic measures to solve the problem. However, to do so would create an equally daunting dilemma. Should Margo Lovegood disappear like the two anonymous women in his past had, it would be front page news and the entire world would hear about it. Ted didn't know if Margo had trusted any of her friends or family with the information on whom she was bedding, but it was a chance he couldn't take. If the police came around to question him about Margo's disappearance, he would have a lot more to worry about than just his political dreams going up in smoke. He could end up in prison for the rest of his life.

It turned out Margo Lovegood was not the only person who delivered a performance worthy of an Oscar that night. At the same time Ted Vargas swore his undying love to her, he was plotting how to kill her without leaving a trace.

Of the handful of close friends Margo Lovegood had in Hollywood, one was an actress quite a few years older than herself.

They had met at a charity event five years before, while Margo was still a virtual unknown. She had inadvertently spilled a glass of wine on a famous country and western singer's shirt. His name was Travis Bullock. Seated beside him was his wife, Hollywood legend, Stormie Banks.

Margo was mortified. She thought they would both be furious with her. In her experience most famous people didn't take well to having drinks dumped on them. She stuttered an apology and thrust a napkin at the man's chest.

To her surprise, the couple had laughed. Stormie turned to her and said, "Don't worry, honey. Being married to me, Travis has had lots of alcohol spilled on him over the years. He's used to it."

They had been friends ever since. Margo appreciated Stormie. She was one of the few people who would remain Margo's friend, even after her star had fallen. She was also just about the only person in Hollywood who Margo really trusted. In fact, Stormie had been quite influential in helping Margo pick the roles that launched her career.

Stormie amassed a fortune during her years as a leading lady. She had spent a great deal of time splattered all over the tabloids because of a rather out of control drinking problem, and was no stranger to the highs and lows of stardom. They met for lunch two or three times a month.

Stormie had a real knack for picking scripts destined to become box office goldmines, so Margo always showed her the ones she was considering.

The week following Margo's latest Oscar win she showed her a script received from long-time Hollywood casting agent, Glenda Michaels. Stormie wrinkled her nose and told her to burn it.

Margo was clearly very distracted and Stormie could tell something was bothering her that had nothing whatsoever to do with the script she had just seen.

She said, "For a lady who just won the gold you sure don't seem very happy. What's wrong, Margo? I suppose it's about a boy, right? Doesn't matter how famous we are, it's always about a boy."

While Margo had always been very discreet about her relationship with Ted, at this point she really needed someone to talk to.

Stormie's own past included a myriad of marriages and high-profile relationships. Margo recalled reading about one of Stormie's shorter unions, rumored to have ended after her new husband threatened to throw her out a window in Spain. With that kind of drama, Stormie was a good choice to confide her troubles to.

Margo suffered a little bit of stability envy at Stormie's current life. All the drama behind her, and a sexy, silver-fox husband who could sure carry a tune.

She asked, "Stormie, have you ever fallen in love with someone you probably shouldn't have?"

Stormie laughed. "Who, me? The queen of the tabloids? Well, maybe once or twice back when I was around your age. Of course, this dates back to right around the time Babylon fell. So tell me, who is this Mister Wrong?"

Margo shared the details of her married lover's resistance to leaving his wife, but had the good sense not to mention his name or the fact that he was a state senator.

Stormie rummaged in her hand bag and produced a business card. She slid it across the table. "Listen, babe. I don't know if this guy is worth the trouble—the married ones usually aren't. But, I don't want to see him derail your career. You don't need any bad press. Don't you know that married men running around with pretty young starlets are tabloid manna from heaven?"

"It won't come to that. I won't let it. We have been extremely careful," Margo argued.

"These things have a way of sneaking through the cracks. One day you are sure no one knows, and the next day there's a grainy picture of you and the forbidden boy canoodling on the front page of the National Enquirer. The damn paparazzi are everywhere."

Margo waved a hand dismissively. "I know, but we have been very discreet."

Stormie shook her head. "No one is ever as discreet as they think they are. Tomorrow this lunch date will probably be memorialized in some magazine at the check stand where you buy your tampons. The headline will scream that you and I are lovers. There's been a photographer hiding behind a minivan and snapping pictures of us for the last half hour. Did you know that?"

Margo frowned. "I saw him. Like you said, the little weasels are everywhere." She insisted again, "Trust me. No one knows about the affair."

"Yeah? Well, Lord knows, if you were considering a film cast by that bitch Glenda Michaels, you can't be thinking too clearly." Stormie shuddered as she remembered throwing a script and hitting Glenda Michaels in the face with it a few years back.

She shook off the unwanted memory and pointed to the card she had slid across the table. "I never thought I would refer anyone to Belda, but you should give this lady a call. She can help with pretty much anything. She's a scary old bird...but effective. Tell her your love-life woes and she can probably fix them right up. Make the guy leave his wife and love you forever, if that's really what you want…Then later, once you realize what a colossal mistake he was, I'll help with your divorce. I have lots of good lawyers."

Margo laughed and looked at the card curiously. "What is she, like a psychic?" Margo asked.

Stormie grimaced. "Not exactly. More of a bruja. A very expensive bruja. Do you know what that is?"

Margo smiled. "Yep. Someone the rich hire when love just ain't enough. Thanks, Stormie."

The next day Margo Lovegood was on a plane bound for Seattle. If Stormie Banks had known her friend was going to ask Belda for a great deal more than just a love potion, she would have thought twice before she handed her that card.

In fact, if Stormie had any memory of the last potion Belda concocted for her she never would have recommended Bella Luna and their poison prescriptions to anyone. The final potion she'd purchased from Belda nearly ruined Stormie's life and drove her to suicide. Belda had seen to it that all the events surrounding that dark time had been completely erased from Stormie's mind.

That toxic and nearly lethal brew was the reason Belda gave up the reins to Gabriella and went into almost total retirement. It had scared the potion mistress half to death.

One tiny mistake made on the final elixir Stormie purchased had nearly cost Belda everything. She would never forget the actress, or the cursed concoction she had prepared for her.

Margo Lovegood was looking for a far more permanent solution to her romantic woes than just Ted Vargas leaving his wife.

She realized with the Whitehouse looming in the distance, he would never get a divorce. Despite what Ted told her, she saw the way his eyes lit up when he spoke about the presidency. They didn't light up that way when he spoke of Francine. Margo now understood it was not his marriage standing between them.

In order to keep Ted, she was going to have to share him with something much more demanding than a mere wife. She would have to allow him to continue courting the most jealous mistress of all…power.

Gabriella was uneasy when the beautiful woman entered the shop. While she had been expecting her, it was the last famous actress who came to call at Bella Luna that weighed heavily on her mind this afternoon. Belda was not the only one who would not soon forget Stormie Banks and her unusual potion for restored youth.

Gabby was not anxious to learn what Margo Lovegood wanted. When it came to the rich and entitled it never seemed to end well for any of them. It appeared to Gabriella that the more money someone had, the more unreasonable their demands. They never seemed to understand that despite how limitless the resources, sometimes there were things money simply could not buy.

"Good afternoon, Ms. Lovegood. My name is Gabriella." She reached out to shake the woman's hand and escorted her to the office in the back of the shop.

"Thank you for seeing me on such short notice, but I thought I would be meeting with Belda."

Gabby offered a reassuring smile. "Belda has retired. I will be assisting you today. Would you care for a cup of tea?"

"Coffee please," Margo replied, as though she were placing an order with a waitress at a restaurant.

"I'm sorry, we don't have coffee," Gabby replied apologetically. Inside she bristled.

The woman looked only slightly put out. "Tea will be fine. Thank you," Margo said, taking in the surroundings in the cramped, dimly lit room.

When Gabriella returned with two steaming mugs of tea, Margo sipped hers and murmured, "Mmm. This is really good."

Gabby smiled. "Yes, I have been told I make a mean cup of tea. So, Ms. Lovegood, what brings you to Bella Luna today?"

"Before I tell you why I'm here, I need to know I can count on your absolute discretion. My friend who referred me wouldn't have sent me here if you could not be trusted, but I have to ask."

"We treat everyone's confidences with utmost caution, Ms. Lovegood. You may have complete faith that we will take your secrets to the grave. The only thing we ask in return is for the same courtesy. Should we agree to make a potion for you, you would not be permitted to tell anyone about it. Not ever. Unfortunately, if you break that pact the consequences would be dire."

"A potion?" the actress laughed. "Are you serious? That's what you do? You make potions? Forgive me for laughing, but that seems a little, well, ridiculous."

Gabriella fought a strong wave of dislike for their new client. "I assure you alchemy can be quite effective. However, if you feel it is not the best course of action for you, I understand." She began rising from her chair.

"Wait!" the woman cried and held up a hand. "I'm sorry. I was just taken aback. My friend didn't mention anything about potions. She just said this lady Belda could help me with my problem."

"May I ask what the problem is, Ms. Lovegood?"

Looking slightly embarrassed, the actress replied, "The oldest one in the book. Man troubles."

"Ah, I see. Would you care to elaborate?" Gabriella asked stiffly.

"I am in love with a married man. A very powerful man with political ambitions, so naturally divorce is out of the question. I don't suppose you have a magic potion that can get his wife out of the picture?" Margo laughed nervously.

Gabriella was unfazed. "When you say out of the picture, do you mean dead?"

Margo flinched like she had just been struck. "Jeez. You get right to the point, don't you? Are you telling me you have a potion for that? Killing someone?"

Gabriella shrugged noncommittally.

Margo looked around nervously. "Oh, hell, this place isn't bugged, is it? I'm not going to end up on the evening news, am I?"

"Only if you tell anyone about our little chat today. The media always makes such a fuss when someone with name recognition disappears under mysterious circumstances, don't they?"

Margo gasped. The cool and detached tone with which the weird young lady before her delivered that threat sent a chill through her bones. She knew Gabriella was not joking, and she also knew she had come to the right place to solve her problem.

Margo offered a wintry smile. "There is no need to threaten me. You don't honestly think I would tell anyone I just put out a hit on a former judge, do you? Now let's talk about this potion."

"Very well. You accept the terms, Ms. Lovegood?"

"Of course. I won't tell a soul, and I believe you won't either. So, what is our next step? Do we cut our pinkies and swear it in blood, girlfriend?" She wiggled one pinkie in the air.

Gabriella was not amused. Unsmiling, she replied, "That won't be necessary. Now, do you have a way to administer the potion to your romantic rival, or is this something we will need to accomplish for you? Of course, if we have to do it there will be an additional fee. Added risk, you understand."

"I don't even know the woman. I've never met her. I will pay the extra fee for you to do it. So, how much are we talking here?" Margo asked.

A price was quoted and the two women shook hands. While Margo Lovegood wrote out the check, Gabriella asked her for the name of the woman she wanted eliminated.

Upon hearing the name Gabriella's eyes widened in shock.

Once Gabriella saw Margo Lovegood out of the shop, she locked the door behind her and turned the sign to Closed. She quickly ran up the stairs to Belda's apartment and rapped urgently at the door. When Belda opened it, Gabriella rushed inside without waiting for an invitation. "I think we may have a problem, Belda," she declared breathlessly.

Belda smiled benignly. "Gabby, what has you in such a state? I am sure whatever the crisis is we can fix it."

"Why is it that every time we get a famous actress for a client, we are the ones who end up with all the drama?" Gabby moaned.

Belda's eyes narrowed as she was once again reminded of the Stormie Banks fiasco. "Please tell me this one doesn't wish to be young again."

"Oh no, she's quite youthful. What she wants really isn't the issue. It's who the target is that might be a problem."

"What is the name of our new client, Gabby? Who is this actress?"

"Margo Lovegood."

To Gabriella's surprise, Belda laughed. "Oh my, this does complicate things."

"What's so funny, Belda?" Gabby asked suspiciously.

"Am I correct in assuming Ms. Lovegood has enlisted our help to remove her lover's wife, Francine Vargas?" Belda asked.

Gabby nodded her head slowly. "That's right. So, let me get this straight. The wife hired us to take out the mistress? And now the mistress has hired us to take out the wife? This is unbelievable."

Belda smiled. "It certainly is a first. Forgive me for seeing the humor in it."

Gabriella grimaced. "Sure, as long as you forgive me for not finding it nearly as amusing as you do. Belda, what do we do? We can't take them both out. Can we?"

"No, that seems rather unethical, doesn't it? What do you think is the best way to solve this little conundrum, dear?"

Gabby shrugged. "I don't know. The Vargas woman was here first, and besides, she is the wife. I guess we should probably get rid of the actress. I could just tear up Lovegood's check after the job is done... Although, she wouldn't really notice the money missing at that point, now would she?"

Belda shook her head. "Gabriella, we are not thieves. I would never dream of taking money for a potion and then not giving the client what they paid for. No, I believe there is only one fair and equitable way to solve this dilemma."

Part III: The Politician

Nicholas Aguilar had no trouble knocking the limousine driver out and dragging his body into the bushes. He quickly pulled the man's chauffeur's cap from his head and donned it at a rakish angle. The driver would be out for about two hours, so Nicholas had enough time to finish the unpleasant task Belda had assigned him this evening. The car would be back before the chauffeur even came to. And if everything went according to plan, Nicholas would be back in Seattle and asleep in Gabriella's arms by sunrise.

He climbed behind the wheel of the limo and waited for his fare to emerge from the upscale Beverly Hills hotel. Once the man arrived, leaving the actress alone upstairs, he would get this job done as quickly as possible. *Ugh,* he thought to himself. *Another actress.*

Senator Ted Vargas walked quickly out the front door of the hotel, his head down and dark glasses covering his eyes, despite the lateness of the hour.

Nicholas jumped from the car and pulled open the back door for the senator. Once he was situated behind the wheel the glass partition separating him from the passenger in back slid silently open.

"Who the hell are you? Where's Louis?" the senator asked, a worried frown settling on his face.

"Good evening, sir," Nicholas replied in a professional tone, "I'm afraid Louis fell ill. My name is Nick. I will be covering for him this evening."

Ted grumbled, "I don't like this. Louis is always my driver when I am here in Los Angeles. When did he get sick? He was fine when he dropped me off a couple hours ago."

"I'm sorry, sir, I really don't know. I was just told to come pick you up by the service. Where would you like me to take you?"

Ted Vargas looked uncomfortably out the window. He barked, "LAX. And step on it, I have a flight to catch."

"Yes, sir," Nicholas replied and closed the glass partition between them.

Ted Vargas's body was found in Beverly Gardens Park the following morning. The conclusion by local law enforcement was that it was a robbery gone bad. The politician's expensive watch was missing, and his wallet was found a few feet from the body with no cash inside. There was a surveillance camera at the entrance to the park where the senator's body was found with a single gunshot wound to the head, but the tape was mysteriously blank.

Equally mysterious was what on earth Ted Vargas was doing in California. He had no business scheduled there that his secretary was aware of. She did not even know he had left town. When his tearful wife was questioned, she claimed to have no idea what he was doing there either.

The following week, after the senator was laid to rest, a box containing a book entitled *The Spiritual Journey of Dealing with Grief* was delivered to Francine Vargas's home. Folded inside the book was a receipt for a wire transfer that was sent to a private account Francine held in the Cayman Islands. The return address on the package was the Bella Luna Bookstore in Seattle. There was a condolence card with a brief note at the bottom advising her to call again should she require any further assistance.

Margo Lovegood was still very much alive. Francine never called Bella Luna again. She was quite surprised that the strange old woman had returned all the money she paid her, or for that matter, that she had the insight to realize with Ted gone Francine no longer needed the actress out of the way.

Francine accepted the story of the robbery. Though she found the circumstances surrounding her husband's murder odd, she honestly believed karma had just finally caught up with him.

Besides Margo Lovegood, Francine was the only person alive who knew what Ted was doing in California on the day he was murdered. She was quite sure the actress would never utter a word about her relationship with Ted to anyone. The last thing she wanted was that kind of press. Francine marveled that the slut had managed to avoid all negative publicity during her rise to stardom.

She and Ted must have been very careful. It was no small wonder that not a single snapshot of them ever found its way into the papers, via one over-zealous paparazzi hiding behind a bush somewhere.

Francine knew if the police ever found out about her relationship with Ted, Margo Lovegood would become their prime suspect.

For all Francine knew, Margo had killed him. Maybe he tried to break it off with her and things got out of control. It was certainly possible, given how close they were to announcing his run for the presidency. Margo was a dangerous loose end Ted should have snipped long before now.

Francine really didn't care who fired the gun that ended Ted's life. She was convinced her husband's murder was karma. Whose finger actually pulled the trigger was irrelevant. The bastard got what he had coming to him. True, if she'd been given the choice, thirty years of infidelity would have caught up with Ted about a decade later. But, who was she to question fate?

While she would always hate Margo Lovegood the same way she hated all of Ted's mistresses, she no longer wanted the woman dead. Francine never had any interest in causing harm to any of her husband's paramours—and she knew about each and every one of them. She'd had a slew of private investigators on retainer for years. The pictures were all safely kept in a safe deposit box Ted knew nothing about. Just in case he ever got sloppy and she needed them for leverage during a divorce.

Francine never sought Belda's assistance to eliminate Margo Lovegood for something so trifling as jealousy. She just couldn't bear to watch some tramp half her age destroy everything she had spent the last thirty years building.

Of course, her dreams of becoming First Lady were all gone now anyway, and it wasn't even the actress's fault. Someday, when the sting wasn't quite so sharp, Francine thought she might be able see the irony in it all.

Fortunately, for now, the several million dollars in life insurance she carried on her husband dulled the pain quite nicely.

When the phone rang at Bella Luna two days after Senator Vargas's funeral, Gabriella was not surprised to hear Margo Lovegood's sultry voice on the line.

"Is it too late for me to change my mind?" the actress asked.

Gabriella assured her it wasn't. She offered condolences on the passing of Ms. Lovegood's friend, and promised to tear up her check.

Gabriella supposed Belda had done the right thing, but they sure lost an awful lot of money on those two women. "Actresses," Gabby grumbled, "Bloody actresses. Nothing but trouble."

She picked up Eros and stroked him beneath the chin.

Though Belda could have kept both women's money, and just as easily completed the tasks they had paid for, she decided on a different course of action. While her moral compass might be suspect to some, Belda's conscience was clear.

She believed the greater good would be served by not honoring either woman's wishes. By killing Ted Vargas—the true source of both of their misery, Belda was convinced she had saved an entire country from peril.

If Ted Vargas had lived, he almost certainly would have been elected president, regardless of whether or not his wife or his mistress died. Belda believed the country had suffered enough during certain previous administrations. She could well imagine the havoc Ted Vargas would have wreaked on an unsuspecting world. The damage which could be done by a man as corrupt and manipulative as Ted Vargas was unfathomable.

Perhaps, Belda believed, things would have turned out better for an entire nation, had she been given the opportunity to rewrite history several years earlier.

While she gave up a great deal of money when she decided it was Ted Vargas who needed to go instead of the two women in his life, she did not mind. Belda believed sometimes one must make sacrifices, so good may triumph over evil.

What Readers are saying...

Other Books By Krystal Lawrence

Risen

Risen II – The Progeny

Be Careful What You Wish For

About The Author

Krystal is the author of three previous novels and numerous short stories. She lives in the Pacific Northwest.

Visit the author's website:
http://www.darksidestories.com

About the Artist

Kira Sokolovskaia was born in Moscow, Russia. She graduated with a degree in graphic arts. Kira has earned a reputation as one of the premiere artists in the Vancouver area, where she lives with her husband and son. Her paintings have been purchased by collectors and sought after worldwide. Kira specializes in pastel paintings, illustrations and pen and ink drawings.

You can view Kira's work at: kir-za.tumblr.com

CPSIA information can be obtained
at www.ICGtesting.com
Printed in the USA
BVOW03*1132231116

R7634300001B/R76343PG467998BVX1B/1/P